<u>LOVE NOTES</u>

A
Mimi Patterson/Gianna
Maglione Mystery

PENNY MICKELBURY

LOVE NOTES

A Mimi Patterson/Gianna Maglione Mystery

migibooks

A division of
48/52 Development Studio
Los Angeles, California
2001

Printed in Canada
First Edition October 2001

Cover photograph and design by Peggy A. Blow for
48/52 Development Studio, Inc.

Mickelbury, Penny, 1948–
Love Notes: A Mimi Patterson/Gianna Maglione
Mystery / by Penny Mickelbury

ISBN 0-9714222-0-6

This book is dedicated to Marianne Basford, bartender *extraordinaire*, who inspired this story. To Peggy Blow, person *extraordinaire*, who inspires everything else. And to loyal, die-hard Mimi/Gianna fans everywhere who never stopped asking when the new Mimi/Gianna book was coming, and who never despaired that it would.

PROLOGUE

Washington, D.C.

It was a dream come true, fantasy become reality, that she, Ellie Litton, could be in this city, strolling the monument grounds on a chilly Fall evening, leaves swirling and crunching beneath her feet, sun setting over the Potomac, Iowa so distant as to be practically non-existent in her consciousness. It was not a stretch to call it a miracle, she thought; after all, she had saved her own life, as surely as if some divine intervention had cured her of a terminal sickness.

She resisted the urge to pinch herself. She had black and blue marks from so many pinches during this week while she waited for her new reality to take hold and replace the old. She'd always done that: pinched herself. Sometimes— like recently— it was to confirm the reality of her presence in some surreal situation or circumstance; but more often, in the past, she had squeezed some secret skin between thumb and forefinger to prevent herself from screaming in anger or frustration or misery or whatever described the lifetime of feelings that she'd spent her life suppressing with painful pinches. But that was all in the past; she wasn't at home in Iowa, wallowing in misery and fantasizing an

1

escape. Iowa no longer was home, and her escape was a done deal. She was in Washington, D.C., the nation's capital— the capital of the free world— strolling on a world-famous boulevard, surrounded by government workers rushing to subways and busses and home, and tourists going no place in a hurry. Like herself. Except she wasn't a tourist and this, her first visit to Washington, actually was a home-coming of sorts. After a week in D.C., soaking up the history and culture of the place and reveling in her new freedom, she would move to her new home in Columbia, Maryland, a sleek, middle-to-upper crust enclave situated equidistant between D.C. and Baltimore. She could claim either city as home, depending on her mood. "Any place but Des Moines," she said out loud, and then looked around to make sure no one had heard her talking to herself. Another habit she'd no longer need: talking out loud to herself because she was the only person who'd listen to what she had to say. Those days were over. "Thank God!"

She clutched the tourist map though she no longer needed to refer to it. She knew exactly where she was. The map's details were burned into her memory, so many times had she gazed at it, studied it, mesmerized by the history that had come to be real life for her these last days. She was walking east on Constitution Avenue. The State Department was across the street, in the neighborhood called Foggy Bottom. The Reflecting Pool was ahead, on her right; she'd see it as she walked past it, though she wouldn't have time to stop and...reflect. She didn't want to be late for her rendezvous at the steps of the Lincoln Memorial and she knew if she stopped at the Reflecting Pool she'd be there a while. That already was a habit, like spending much longer than planned at the Vietnam Memorial, though she wasn't regretful about that, not in the least. She'd found his name— her oldest brother's— etched there in the shiny black stone: **ELDEN LITTON**. Alive forever, the name of the older brother dead so many years now, killed in a foreign war that few people seemed to care about anymore. She had touched his name, moved her finger

2

across the carved letters, and closed her eyes and tried to remember what he looked like. She could not. After all, he'd been dead for almost thirty-six years. She was just fourteen when he went off to war, the baby of the family and the only girl, and she had not understood that she should have said good- bye to him; had not known it was possible he'd never come home again. She surprised herself that first day at the black Wall by weeping at the thought, and compounded her surprise by not feeling at all self-conscious about such a public display of emotion. She wasn't the only one crying, and even if she had been, it would have been all right. She was entitled to her feelings, and to express them. She tightened her grip on the rolled up map in her hand, as if holding on to her entitlement. It was new to Ellie; as new as her chic, expensive wardrobe, as new as the house she owned, as new as the freedom to stroll at twilight on Constitution Avenue in Washington, D.C., en route to meet her new lover.

She found herself caught up in a swirl of tourists leaving the Museum of Natural History and, like an unsuspecting insect snared in a spider's web, she moved along with them, not annoyed or intimidated by their frenetic energy, and she marveled at the growth that had occurred within her. She really was a different person— one who could and would call her mother tonight and tell the old woman about Elden's name on the Wall. Since she couldn't tell her about Elvis's name on the quilt. Elvis, her favorite brother, dead of AIDS, alone and ashamed and afraid. Ellie, ostensibly in Chicago on business, but there really to see the Quilt and Elvis's name on it. She had sewn the panel herself, and sent it to be included. And it was there! She recalled feeling a strange, odd pride, just as she had at the Vietnam Memorial. Her brothers— the eldest and the youngest— were dead, but their names would live for ever. Her mother wouldn't have wanted to hear about Elvis's name memorialized in the Quilt, but she'd care about Elden's name carved into the black Wall. Maybe that would take the edge of the other news, that she, Ellie, would not be returning to Iowa. Ever. There was no sadness within her, no

3

pang of regret at how the news would affect her mother. She was fifty years old. It was time to leave home, time to exit her mother's sphere of influence and control, time to stop being the dutiful daughter— the dutiful, only daughter without husband and children whose job it was to care for her widowed, elderly mother. No matter that she held down a full time job with enormous responsibility and that none of her sisters-in-law worked outside the home. "Time for you to take care of yourself, Mom. Or get one of your precious sons or their precious wives to take care of you. I'm busy having a life now."

She had spoken aloud again, and the swiftness with which the amiable crowd that surrounded her turned hostile and moved away was startling. "Guess it's not a good idea to talk to yourself out loud in D.C.," she said, just as sudden gust of cold air whipped across the monument grounds. One of the women in the tourist group emitted a long, shrill, "Oooooo!" and wrapped her arms around herself. She wore a cotton skirt and tee shirt— not the proper attire for Washington in October. Her comrades laughed and enveloped her in a group hug and, like a giant bug-body with many legs, they scurried up the street. Ellie was toasty in her wool-blend slacks and sweater from Nordstrom. She'd read up on D.C. weather and knew that it could turn sharply colder in October, though it wouldn't last long so early in the season.

She enjoyed possessing such knowledge. It meant she wouldn't look like a stupid tourist. The propriety of her wardrobe marked her a resident of the area; their expense designated her successful. She was a talented enough software designer that she'd been scooped up almost immediately by a Maryland engineering firm after posting her resume on the internet. One month she decided to leave Iowa and the next month she had a new job, a new house, a new car. And a new lover. She twisted the ring on her baby finger and rubbed it like a talisman.

Ellie stepped off the sidewalk onto the thick grass and angled toward the Potomac. She felt more alive, more excited, more anticipatory, than at any other time in her life. Whoever

4

said, "Life begins at forty," deserved an award for Biggest Understatement of Fact. "Better late than never," she said to herself, for she was alone in her approach to Mr. Lincoln, and she didn't wonder why. It definitely was chillier this close to the water, and much darker. The museums and monuments were closed for the night, the tourists all somewhere warm. "I've got this all to myself." She spread her arms wide and embraced the vista. She had wondered at first, but now she understood why the Lincoln Memorial was the perfect choice for a romantic assignation at dusk on a chilly night. Here beside the Potomac, which drifted lazily toward Virginia and, ultimately, into the Chesapeake Bay, with the planes headed toward the airport hanging low in the sky, circling, waiting their turn to land, their lights flashing almost impatiently— here it was serene and lovely and private. Here, she could be kissed and fondled and no one would see. No one but him, and he didn't care: Abraham Lincoln, grim and silent, bathed in golden light. She gazed at the solemn visage of the sixteenth president and silently declared her own emancipation.

Suddenly, a sharply colder wind cut across the path leading to Mr. Lincoln and Ellie shivered and leaned into it. "That felt like Iowa," she said to herself with a laugh. "D.C., don't you deceive me!"

She was still laughing when the garrote buried itself in the folds of her neck and severed her esophagus.

CHAPTER ONE

Mimi Patterson hated the ringing of the telephone in the middle of the night more than just about anything else, so when it rang at 3:44 on that Friday morning she pulled the pillow over her head and burrowed more deeply beneath the covers and snuggled more closely into the spoon that was Gianna.

Gianna Maglione awoke fully alert at the late-night ringing of the phone, but this wasn't her phone. It was Mimi's. Gianna picked it up in the middle of the third ring, pulled the pillow from Mimi's head, and placed the receiver against her ear. "Answer the phone, Mimi."

"'Lo?" Mimi whispered.

"Goddammit, Patterson, get your ass up and get it in here!" the voice on the other end bellowed.

Mimi groaned and pushed the phone away, toward Gianna, who heard, loudly and clearly, "You hear me, Patterson? I said get you ass in here! Fuckin' David Trimble splattered his fuckin' brains all over his living room wall and his wife says it's your fuckin' fault! She's suing you, the paper, half the goddam editors, and God only knows who else! Goddammit, get your ass in here, Patterson, and deal with this mess you made! I've got a desk to run."

The line went dead and Gianna replaced the phone in its stand. She sat up, turned on the light, and looked down at the covered-up lump that was her lover. The pillow was back over her head and she was in a fetal ball. Gianna snatched the pillow away and pulled back the covers. It took about two seconds for the chill to envelop Mimi's nakedness. Her eyes snapped open.

"What'd you do that for?"

"Did you hear that message?"

"What message?"

"On the telephone, Mimi. Your night editor. Henry's his name, right?"

"Henry called?" Mimi asked, shivering and reaching for covers that Gianna kept just out of reach. "Did I talk to him? What'd he say?"

"No, you didn't talk to him, but I listened to him, and he said for you to get your ass to work because David Trimble committed suicide and his wife is blaming you. She's also suing you and several editors at the paper."

Mimi sat up, shivering but awake. She required just a few seconds to process what Gianna had said and the potential ramifications of the situation. She'd recently completed a series of stories— yet *another* series of stories— on yet *another* corrupt government official. This one, David Trimble, had been, until Mimi's stories got him fired and indicted, the chief financial officer of a county school system in Virginia. Trimble thought of the county's money as his money and he used it to play the stock market as if he were a day trader instead of a civil servant. Trimble proved to be a better trader than he was civil servant, earning close to a million dollars with his county school board stake. He even paid back the money he'd stolen, and thought that should have been sufficient to keep him out of trouble. He'd been livid when, after Mimi's first story, the county supervisors had suspended him, and apoplectic when the SEC stepped in and made it a Federal case, demanding that he relinquish and return the money he'd made in the stock market. "Ill-gotten gains," the prosecutor called the money. "Mine!" Trimble and his wife called it, vehemently denying the theft of any public funds and insisting that they had a right to keep the stock profits.

It wasn't the first series of articles to run under the byline, **M. Montgomery Patterson,** to result in the ruin of a public official, though as far as Mimi was concerned, it easily could be the last. She was tired of corrupt public officials, and even more tired of having the job of exposing their avarice.

Gianna knew the story and the facts behind it and she

7

watched Mimi ruminate, unable to read the expression on her face. A cop by trade and a lieutenant by rank, she was an expert at reading facial expressions, and knew exactly what it meant when there was nothing to read. But before Gianna could ask what she was thinking, Mimi sighed, shivered again, and hauled herself out of bed, causing in Gianna a sharp pang of regret to accompany the equally sharp pang of desire she always felt at the sight of the lovely, brown body.

"I hate these stories and I'm not doing any more of them." Mimi picked up her robe from the floor at the foot of the bed and put it on, wrapping it tightly around her. "It's already cold and it's still October," she said shivering as she crossed to the closet, opened the door, and grabbed a pair of jeans. "What's December going to be like?"

"What kind of stories will you do, then?" Gianna asked, sensing that she needed to nudge Mimi back to center. That's why Gianna couldn't get a reading: there was none to be gotten, and that occurred only when Mimi was "out of whack," as she called it, when she was flat and emotionless, as she was now.

"None, maybe. How's that sound? I'll get a job at the gym as a personal trainer and fitness expert. Think I'll attract any paying customers?"

Before Gianna could respond, the phone rang and Mimi rushed to answer it. She grabbed it up, her face wrinkled in irritation, and before the receiver met her ear she was shouting into it, "Goddammit, Henry, I'm on my way!" She punched the phone off and threw it down on the bed and, hands on hips, glared evilly at it. "And why the hell is it *my* fault the asshole killed himself? I didn't tell him to steal the money, the stupid, greedy bastard, but I'm the one who gets blamed when he decides he can't live with the consequences of his actions."

Gianna grinned. Mimi was back— *her* Mimi, the one full of passion every waking moment of her life. "I'd pay for your personal attention, but we'll discuss that later. You'd better get yourself to the paper."

8

"I don't know what the rush is all about, they don't need me." She opened the chest of drawers and got a sweater, panties and bra, and socks, then whipped back around to face Gianna. "Here's an idea for a new slogan for the mealy-mouthed, weasley politicians since so many of their dicks have gotten caught in the family values vice: Be a Good American— Try Personal Responsibility. Think it'll fly?"

Gianna frowned. "What do you mean, they don't need you? And why are you wearing jeans to work? And no, it won't fly. That's why something as weasley and mealy-mouthed as family values *does* fly. Now, why do you say they don't they need you?"

"If Trimble's wife is going to sue me— me personally and not just the paper— then I'm off the story because I've become part of the story and I can't cover myself. It'll be assigned to somebody else. Why they want me in now is to see if they can weasel my notes and sources out of me. That's why I'm wearing jeans to work. I won't be going anywhere, and I won't be doing anything but talking to bosses and lawyers. And they'll hate it that I'm wearing jeans. And that my hair is standing all over my head." She looked at herself in the mirror. Her hair was, indeed, standing all over her head— in unruly, curly ringlets that signified that her need of a haircut was at least a month overdue. Gianna secretly loved Mimi's hair that way— in its pre-dreadlock stage— wild and free and totally resistant to the efforts of the comb.

"Can they?" Gianna asked, trying to remain focused on the business about notes and sources instead of on Mimi's appearance. Which Gianna found more than a little alluring, even at four o'clock in the morning.

"Hell no," Mimi snapped. "This is a brand new story and whoever's assigned to it can develop their own sources."

"Then why wake you up at such an ungodly hour?"

"Because," Mimi responded, "lawyers hate it when reporters become part of the story. Personalizing the First

9

Amendment muddies the waters. It's no longer an abstraction when a reporter or editor's name is attached to a noble concept. Or to a lawsuit." She disappeared into the bathroom and Gianna heard the shower start. Shivering in her own nakedness, she slid her feet into her slippers, found her own robe at the foot of the bed, and headed for the kitchen. She had coffee made and in the thermos by the time Mimi was ready to walk out the door.

"Are you in for a really hard time?" she asked, kissing the back of her neck and further mussing her unruly mop of hair.

Mimi shook her head and the ringlets danced. "The hardest thing I'll have to do today is stay awake while I talk to the lawyers and not yawn in their faces. I'm already envisioning myself back in bed tonight and deeply asleep before the news comes on."

"Uh, uh," Gianna said, shaking her head. "Not tonight, my sweet."

"And why not tonight?" Mimi whipped around to face Gianna, almost dropping her thermos in an effort to keep from dropping her purse, which hit the garage floor, spilling its contents. And as she cursed under her breath and shoved pens, a notepad and an eyeglasses case back into her purse, Gianna reminded her that they'd promised to attend the grand opening party of the new women's bar on Capitol Hill.

"You promised Marianne and Renee you'd be there and they'll be really hurt if you're not. Especially Marianne. You know how personally she takes rejection."

"She'll get over it," Mimi said uncharitably, tossing her belongings into the car and climbing in behind them.

"You're going, Mimi. We don't have to stay late, but you're going." Gianna blew her a kiss and closed the kitchen door as the car door slammed shut, thereby missing Mimi's reaction to her pronouncement, though she could easily imagine what that reaction was. Before crawling back into bed, she called Mimi's office and left a sweet message on her voicemail. She checked the clock to be certain the alarm was set, turned off the light, and returned to sleep as easily as she'd woken from it.

Mimi's jaw muscles worked with the effort to stifle the yawn that had been threatening to escape for the last half hour. The six men seated at the table with her were waiting for her to answer a question that she'd answered twice already. Three of the men were the newspaper's lawyers and three of them were editors and all of them, ostensibly, were on her side in this matter. Yet, she was having a difficult time feeling allied with them. Where was the woman lawyer? Where was the woman editor? And the fact that one of the lawyers and one of the editors was Black provided Mimi with no sense of comfort, and she wondered if that were deliberate on their part. Were they letting her know that she could expect no special protection or sanction from them just because she was Black? Good thing she had no expectations.

It was much too warm in the conference room; it was too warm in the entire building. The unexpected and early winter-like weather had kicked on the central heat and that smell that accompanied the first heat of the season permeated the air, made Mimi's nose tingle. Perhaps a sneeze would go over better than a yawn. Or she could just put her head down on the table, close her eyes, and go to sleep.

"I've answered that question twice, but they say the third time's the charm, so here goes. David Trimble did absolutely, positively and without a doubt, refuse to talk to me before my story ran. I left messages on his home answering machine and with his wife. I left messages on his office voice mail and with the receptionist. I sent registered letters to his home and to his office. David Trimble never responded. And if he had, what difference would it have made?" She looked directly at her immediate boss as she asked the question and he shifted in his seat and shifted his gaze across the table to one of the lawyers. Wassily was his name, weasel was his game.

"Mimi, we just want to make certain we have all the facts," the lead lawyer said, smiling at her. He was the only one of the lawyers who talked. The other two wrote on their yellow legal pads, even when nobody was talking.

"You have them," she said. "Can I go now?"

"I don't think you understand the gravity of this situation," her boss, the Weasel, said, a hint of a whine in his voice. "A man is dead and his widow is blaming you, and me, and this newspaper."

"I didn't kill him. Did you?"

The lead lawyer raised his hands, palms out. "Let's keep tempers under control, please, and keep to the facts. And the fact is, a lawsuit like this one puts the paper in a bad light, Mimi, and it's our job to do as much damage control as possible."

Mimi imitated the lawyer's gestures, raising her hands and smiling. "I'm all for that, guys, and as I see it, there are only two ways to control the damage. First, all the David Trimble-like weenies stop stealing the public's money, or, second, we in the press ignore them when they do. If we don't rat 'em out, then they won't have to blow their brains out when they get caught." She looked around the table, meeting all six pairs of the eyes that were locked on hers, anger in every pair. "Either way is fine with me. What's not fine is having you try to shift the blame to me."

"Nobody's trying to shift the blame to you, Mimi," the lawyer said.

"Sure you are," Mimi responded. "Otherwise, this would have been handled over the phone. This isn't my first law suit but it is the first time six of you have ganged up on me behind closed doors, and I want you to know that I don't like it. Not one little bit."

The Weasel looked at his boss and then at Mimi. "We're not ganging up on you, Mimi, we're merely trying to keep you in the loop and part of the process. If there's going to be a huge public outcry in response to Trimble's death, you're going to be affected just as we are, and we need to fashion a proper response."

Mimi stood up. "I don't need to fashion anything and you don't need to fashion anything for me. I did my job. I did it

12

honestly and truthfully and without breaking any canons or ethics of my profession." She looked directly at the lead lawyer. "Or of yours."

Inside *The Bayou*, it could have been Mardi Gras, or Halloween, or the free-at-last party for the winner of the lottery, or a reprise of the world-wide millennium celebration. Or a combination of all of them— that's how seriously the revelers were taking the opening of the new women's bar/restaurant/dance club/piano bar. By the best recollection of the most social of D.C.'s social butterflies, it had been more than twenty years since a new women's gathering spot had debuted in the nation's capital— a *real* women's bar, not some hybrid thing that catered to straights a couple of nights a week, to men a couple of nights a week, and to different ethnicities of women the other nights. *The Bayou* was the real thing: a bar for the committed imbibers; a restaurant specializing in genuine— and expensive— Louisiana cuisine for the epicures; a game room for the players; a good sized dance floor the energetic; and a cozy piano bar for the romantics. The place looked like it belonged on the water. It had rafters and railings and lots of glass and a plank floor. And at the moment, more women than Mimi and Gianna could remember seeing in one place in a very long time. All kinds of women, all ages of women, all sizes and shapes and colors of women, all of them surrendering to full enjoyment of the moment.

"Aren't you glad you came?" Gianna yelled into her ear, the only way to be heard over the din.

Mimi shrugged, grinned and nodded. She *was* glad she'd come. A party was exactly what she needed to shake off the awfulness of her day. She tried to lead Gianna to the dance floor, and was definitively rebuffed. Gianna didn't dance. Ever. Mimi did, whenever she got the chance, so she waved good-bye, melted into the crowd, and, the rhythm of the room permeating her bones, made her way to the dance floor. She hadn't been dancing in so long she couldn't remember the last time, and for a moment

13

she was saddened by the thought. How could she deprive herself of something she enjoyed so much? Then she reminded herself that until the opening of *The Bayou,* there was no place she'd have wanted to spend an evening dancing. But that was then and this was now, and right now the music ruled and Mimi was a willing and loyal subject. She took to the floor— no partner necessary. Or so she thought. Two couples turned away from her when she danced into their sphere— all four of the women young, tatooed, and earringed. Mimi was so shocked that she stopped moving and stood looking in amazement at the four young women as they danced away from her, apparently never having given her a second thought. She moved, finally, when she was bumped and jostled by the other dancers; but she moved to get out of the way, not to dance. She'd lost the desire for that.

The crowd was thick as raw honey and Mimi had no choice but to flow with it as it oozed toward the far edge of the dance floor. That's when she spied Marianne and Renee, in the throes of some wild, crazy gyrations that might have been dancing on some other planet where rhythm wasn't essential to movement. Her irritation of a few moments ago forgotten, she shimmied over and wrapped an arm around each of them.

"Mimi!" they shrieked in delight, each landing a kiss on her each of her cheeks. They were so genuinely glad to see her that she experienced another pang of sadness at the thought that had Gianna listened to her, she wouldn't have been here. They pulled her into their wild and crazy dance and, in a matter of seconds, several other women had joined the mad whirl. In seconds, she'd shaken off every ugly emotion she'd experienced during the day, including being snubbed by the baby dykes. She'd much rather dance with Marianne and Renee and the half dozen other women who gyrated with them for several minutes before moving off to join other groups. This, Mimi thought as she closed her eyes and felt the beat of the music in her veins, is how dancing is supposed to happen.

"Where's Gianna?" she heard in her ear, and opened her

14

eyes to find herself cheek-to-cheek with Marianne. The decibel count was increasing by the minute, and the only way to be heard was to yell directly into an ear.

Mimi leaned in even closer to answer. "Probably shooting pool." Marianne and Gianna had been friends for half their lives and Marianne knew how Gianna felt about dancing. "Gianna's why we have a game room here," Marianna yelled into Mimi's ear, and then she and Renee were enveloped by another group of merrymakers and Mimi was carried back toward the middle of the dance floor, this time to be welcomed by people who knew how to appreciate a serious dancer like herself; people, she realized, who had achieved the age of reason. She could make this a habit, she thought as she whirled around. And she'd have time for such habitual pleasures now that she no longer would be obsessed with her work— a decision she'd made after her meeting that morning. She'd be damned if she was going to do their dirty work and also be their pariah. If the public didn't care that their government officials were corrupt, who was she to carry the flag up the hill? She'd been ferreting out graft and corruption long enough. Let somebody else do it. She'd happily work an eight-hour, five day week and become a *Bayou* regular. Hell, she'd probably have to; just because she'd decided to opt for normality didn't mean Gianna would follow. What would she do with herself all those extra hours if she wasn't working and Gianna was?

She burned up the floor for the next hour, encountering more than a dozen friends and acquaintances in the process, some of them people she hadn't seen in years, half of them asking about Beverly, her former lover. She definitely needed to get out more. She and Bev had split up three years ago, and she'd been with Gianna for over a year, and people she'd known for a decade didn't know about either of those changes in her life. She made two dinner dates for the following weekend, to renew old friendships and to introduce Gianna to those friends, and a breakfast date with the new artistic director of a theater company whose work she admired. Then she set out to find Gianna.

Easier said than done. It was midnight and a female body occupied every inch of space in *The Bayou*. Ordinarily, not a bad thing. But when one woman is searching for another woman and the only visual targets are women, well, the search may prove interesting if not immediately successful. Mimi thought she spied Gianna at least five times, and mumbled to herself that, "You'd think I know what she looks like by now," and she was about to give up and go search, instead, for food when she saw Gianna huddled in a corner with Marianne. They were standing very close together and leaning toward each other, heads touching. They'd have to stand that close, Mimi knew, to hear each other over the crowd noise. But it was their facial expressions that grabbed Mimi's attention, especially Gianna's. She wore her "lieutenant look." And it wasn't just that her expression was grave or that her attention was focused entirely on what Marianne was saying. Gianna's eyes were in another place, in the place where she saw ugliness and evil and hatred. In the place where she was a cop.

Mimi shuddered. What could Marianne know that could transport the head of the D.C. Police Department's Hate Crimes Unit into that space? She watched Gianna listen. She was perfectly still, yet her body radiated kinetic energy, and Mimi knew that whatever Marianne was saying was both important and serious, because she would never intrude on Gianna's professional self in this kind of environment otherwise, and if it were some frivolous matter, Gianna never would give it this kind of attention. She watched them for several seconds more, then headed for the restaurant. It was hours past dinner time and when she saw the line leading to the food, she knew it easily would be another hour before she'd be able to quell her ravenous hunger. Or maybe it was just the idea of genuine Creole and Cajun food that inspired the instant and overwhelming desire to eat. Her stomach rumbled.

"Me, too," she heard from behind her. She turned to face

a tiny, very pretty woman with close-cropped hair and oversized eyeglasses with dark tinted lenses that dwarfed her face. She looked vaguely familiar.

"Well, we'd both better find some mind over matter techniques to help us survive this line," Mimi replied equably.

"No shit, Sherlock," her companion responded with a dry, dead-pan tone, and Mimi knew instantly who she was: Cassandra Ali, a member of Gianna's Hate Crimes Unit. She'd been on a medical leave of absence since being brutally beaten and almost raped by a neo-Nazi asshole almost a year ago. Gianna had broken several small bones in her hand punching out the scum who'd beat the young cop. Cassandra had lost the sight in her left eye and though she had otherwise recovered physically, she still was severely emotionally traumatized, and Mimi knew that Gianna worried about her; worried whether Cassandra Ali ever could return to full-time active duty.

"You look familiar," Cassie said as Mimi was wondering whether— and how— to make herself known. "My name's Cassie," Cassie said, extending her hand and removing the need for speculation.

"Mimi Patterson," Mimi answered, offering her hand in return, and watching the recognition dawn in the other woman's eyes.

"The Italian lieutenant's woman," Cassie said with a slightly mocking smile that didn't quite make it all the way to her eyes. "Is she here?"

Mimi nodded. "She's over there somewhere," she replied, waving her arm in the direction where she'd last seen Gianna.

"I'm surprised. I didn't think she was this out."

"She's not," Mimi answered, "but Marianne and Renee are good friends and she wanted to be supportive."

Cassie smiled, and Mimi for the first time noticed the damaged left eye behind the dark lenses. "That's the kind of thing the lieutenant would do, put her own rep on the line to support her friends."

17

Mimi heard a slight bitterness in the tone, and decided not to respond. Instead, she watched Cassie think and decide whether to speak further. Then she realized that they weren't yelling at each other. Leaving the dance floor and entering any of the side rooms— restaurant, game room, or piano bar— resulted in dramatic reduction of the noise level. So, instead of being deafening, the sound of a couple of hundred or so ravenous women lined up, waiting to eat, was merely cacophonous. Cassie was not uncomfortable being observed or being quiet. Gianna once told Mimi that she thought of Cassie as the one most like herself, and Mimi could see why she'd think that.

"You're a good reporter," Cassie finally said.

"And I hear you're a good cop."

The comment took Cassie by surprise. Then it annoyed her. Then her face changed and sadness took over. "I was a good cop," she said slowly, as if measuring the words for accuracy. "I could have been one of the best. I was learning from one of the best. But that's all over now." And she walked away. Mimi watched her go and felt her own appetite leave with her.

"Damn," she muttered.

"Lovers' spat?"

Mimi heard the words behind her and turned to find a grinning, vacuous face too close to her own. She strangled the words that were on their way out of her mouth, mean bruising words; words that the grinning, vacuous face didn't deserve; words that more suitably belonged to her editors and the company lawyers, or to the slime that had brutalized Cassie Ali. She, too, left the food line, and, following in Cassie's footsteps, she left the relative quiet of the restaurant to search for Gianna in the crush of bodies and noise.

Gianna bit her ear, then whispered into it, "You're lucky I don't tell the world what a soft touch you are."

"It takes one to know one." Mimi returned the bite, beginning with a nip to the neck and working her way down.

18

When finally she took her mouth from Gianna, she sat up in bed and switched on the light. They were at Gianna's and the lights were on a shelf above the bed, so they could lie with their heads beneath the shelf and see each other without being blinded. "And if I'm a soft touch, what does that make you?" She rolled over into Gianna's arms.

"A connoisseur of soft touches," Gianna answered, softly touching Mimi all over.

"What are you going to do about her?" Mimi asked, unable to hold back the question any longer.

"I don't know," Gianna answered as softly as one of her touches. "I want her back, but she's not ready, and I can't keep an open slot for much longer. They're already cutting budgets out from under department heads, and you know that Hate Crimes has never been anyone's favorite child. I'm still alive right now only because of the good will of the Chief. If he pulls his support, not only is Cassie's place in the Unit history, but the Unit itself is history."

Mimi was quiet. It was rare that Gianna confided so much so readily and she didn't want to push her luck. So, she changed the subject. "Speaking of which, I've asked for a new assignment."

"And what was the answer?" Gianna responded as if she'd known what Mimi was going to say.

"'No', of course. But I don't take 'no' answers with good grace." Mimi sat up, shivered in the chill, then scooted back down under the covers and close to Gianna. "They just need time to adjust to the idea."

"You're too good for them to just let you do something else, Mimi. You know that. Why not just take off a couple of weeks and go back to it fresh and rested? And let that lawsuit business die down."

Mimi sat up again, this time pulling the covers around her shoulders. "Because nothing will change, Gianna. And it's more than just the stupid lawsuit. I don't really give a shit about that.

19

The fool stole the money and then was too big a coward to face the music and do his time."

Gianna sat up, pulling the covers up to her chin. "Then what is it?"

"People," Mimi spat out. "The citizenry," she said with a sneer. "They don't give a damn anymore about graft and corruption in high places. Half of them have come to expect it and think it's normal, and the other half subscribe to some sick notion that whatever anybody can get away with is all right, and that it really is my fault that Trimble killed himself. If it hadn't been for me nosing in *his* affairs, he'd still be alive. After all," she said bitterly, " he *did* repay the money."

Gianna pulled her closer. "I've noticed that the public tends to accept and excuse a lot more illegal behavior. And yes, there is that tendency to blame the messenger. But does that mean you quit? Give up?"

Mimi shrugged. "Why not? I don't want to get used to being sued every time I uncover some dirt, and I definitely don't like being made to feel that it's all my fault. Anyway, I've decided that I could really get into working a forty-hour week. That would give me time to become a regular at *The Bayou,* which would give me time to work on my dance moves."

"And when did you decide all this?"

"If you'd been on the dance floor with me you'd know when. And why. Which reminds me." She threw back the covers, exposing their nakedness to the chilly air. "Get up and feed me!"

"I already did," Gianna whined, grabbing the covers and pulling them all the way back up to her chin.

"I don't mean that," Mimi said, wrapping her robe tightly around herself. "I mean food. I'm starving!"

"How could you be?" Gianna asked, disbelievingly. "It's only been a couple of hours since we ate. Did you work up that much of an appetite?"

"I haven't eaten since this aft...wait a second! Do you

mean to tell me that you ate at *The Bayou?*

"Of course! Didn't you?"

"Did you see that line?" Mimi practically bellowed. "It wrapped twice around the room! And I told you that's where I talked to Cassie Ali, in the stupid line. Or was that one of the many times you weren't listening to me?"

Gianna shook her head at Mimi, as if she'd done something really dumb. "I always listen to you. And why ever would you stand in a line, Mimi?"

"And I suppose you didn't stand in the line?"

"Of course not," Gianna said with a derisive snort as she climbed out of bed and slid into her robe. "Marianne took me into the kitchen. I looked for you, but the crowd was too dense. I had shrimp remoulade and jambalaya and half a catfish po' boy and some red beans and rice and a crawfish something or other— I'd never heard of it— but it was scrumptious! And coffee with chickory in it! Have you ever had that? It's an amazing taste. What is chickory anyway? Think we can buy some to go in our coffee--"

The pillow hit her square in the face.

"Cops!" Mimi said in disgust as she chased Gianna down the hallway to the kitchen. "You get to gorge your face in the kitchen while the rest of us stand in a line that never moves and now I've got to settle for eating spinach ravioli leftovers while you're burping catfish po' boy!"

Gianna stopped and let Mimi catch her. She pulled her into a tight embrace, hands busy beneath the bathrobe. "I'll make it up to you. How's that?"

"How, indeed!" Mimi was struggling to maintain her feigned indignation, was on the brink of giving up the struggle and giving in to Gianna's hands when, a beat after the fact, she picked up on Gianna's teasing tone of voice.

"What did you...you didn't...did you? You did!" She raced past her into the kitchen and flung open the refrigerator door. Three white bags with the newly minted logo of *The Bayou* sat on the top shelf. "Maglione, you're magnificent! I think I'll keep you!"

"I think you'd better," Gianna responded dryly, getting plates from the cabinet. "Who else would have you?"

CHAPTER TWO

The chief of police was Gianna's mentor and her friend, but it was the role of boss that he was playing to the hilt at the moment, making Gianna more angry, miserable— and wary— with every word he spoke. In his youth, the chief had been a Golden Gloves boxer, and he still looked fit enough to climb into the ring with a man half his age. He also still lived up to his ring name of Scrappy, and while he didn't pick fights, he not only never backed away from one but he frequently would escalate a contentious conversation to the level of almost-fight, just so he could win. He liked winning, no matter that an adversary these days never stood a chance against him. He stood in front of his desk, hands stuffed into his pockets and jiggling change, and told her quickly and succinctly what he wanted her to do, knowing she would be angry and waiting for her anger.

She sat facing him, legs crossed at the knee, hands folded in her lap, and held his gaze for several long seconds before looking away. What a way to start a Monday morning. She stood up and turned her back to him so he wouldn't see what was in her eyes, though she knew he'd know anyway. "Why are we sloshing around in this kind of a mess, Chief? This is the business of the Federal authorities."

"It's *my* business, Maglione, when assholes of any stripe— mad bombers or drug dealers or whoever— decide to do their dirt in *my* town. Besides. Think about what I just told you, and play it all the way out to its legal, if not logical, conclusion."

He dropped down into the chair behind his desk and watched her work her way through the situation, which was: He'd received information (and he wouldn't divulge the source of this information) that an offshoot of the Irish Republican Army

23

was based in D.C. and bringing guns in from the southern and southwestern states— where weapons could be purchased easily and legally— for shipment to Ireland; and that a Jamaican drug dealing cartel, also based in D.C., was aware of the Irish group's activities and planned to steal the next consignment of weapons.

Gianna did as ordered, and it didn't take long for her to recognize the potentially bloody nature of such a confrontation; but that wasn't what the Chief wanted her to see. "You think the fight between the FBI and ATF will be worse than the one between the Irish and the Jamaicans." She hadn't asked a question but he nodded his answer.

"You know that old proverb, I don't remember if it's African or Indian, about what happens when two elephants do battle? The grass beneath them get trampled. That's what'll happen to us if the ATF and the Fibbies start pissing on each other over who has jurisdiction. Is it gun running or is it domestic terrorism? And by the time that gets resolved, blood will be flowing in the streets. I won't let that happen."

"But they'll both be mad as hell if they find out you're in the middle of this, Chief, and we'll get trampled anyway."

"I don't give a damn about them being mad. Besides, if you do your job right, Maglione, by the time the Feds find out about it, those guns'll be scrap metal and the mayor'll be kissing my ass for saving his."

Gianna didn't know whether to feel greater sympathy for herself or for her boss, given their predicaments, but there was no doubt about her feelings for Federal agencies. The messes they created, then left for local police departments to clean up when they battled among themselves, were legendary. No local law enforcement agency, big city or little town, was happy to find itself bound to— or burdened by— a Federal presence in a case. The Chief, no doubt, was wedged between the proverbial rock and the hard place. And he wedged her in there with him, for to do what he wanted her to do— which was find the guns before the Jamaicans found them— meant splitting up her team in a

24

way she found distasteful. She was rolling the possibilities around in her brain when the Chief stepped onto her wavelength.

"You want me to let you off this hook, don't you? So you don't have to split your people up along those lines?"

"Why is it me who's on the hook, Chief?"

"Because I don't have anybody else. Because I need somebody I trust, somebody who answers directly to me."

For the better part of a year, Gianna and her Hate Crimes Unit had been, in departmental parlance, Cowboy Cops. That meant they didn't operate under the rules of a chain of command and that Gianna, as a lieutenant, didn't report to a captain. She answered directly and only to the Chief of Police. There were, to her knowledge, three other such units that reported directly to the Chief: immigration, drugs, and the gang and violence task forces. There were rumors of others but no one knew for certain, and the Chief certainly never volunteered any clarifying information. The specialty units enjoyed an enviable amount of freedom to work cases as they needed to be worked, without the oversight of, in Gianna's case, a captain to report and answer to. The down side was the requirement to respond, as now, to an immediate order of the chief, no matter what.

"You've got to find the damn guns before the Jamaicans find them, Maglione. I'll be damned if I'll let a bunch of foreign assholes wreak that kind of havoc on my town! Not as long as I'm the top cop."

"Foreign assholes?" Gianna looked at him in amazement. She'd never heard him say such a thing.

"That's what they are! They're from someplace else and that makes 'em foreign, and they think they can come into this country and raise all kinds of hell and get away with it and that makes 'em assholes. Well, I'm sick of it and I won't stand by and let it happen in my city. Now. You got anything relevant to say?"

"What makes you so certain the guns are here? I've never heard of any IRA activity in this area."

"Technically, it's not the IRA you're familiar with, it's an off-shoot, a group that wants the peace process to fail. And they're definitely here," he said, and something in his tone caused her to take a hard look at him.

"Is there something you're not telling me, Chief?"

He managed a little laugh. "There's always something I'm not telling you, Maglione, and I ain't ever gonna tell you everything I know. But suppose you tell me how you plan to work this thing, now that you've had time to think about it."

"Now that I've had time to...are you kidding?"

"I'm not, and I'm waiting."

She shook her head at him. What a crafty bastard he was. "Eric and Tim on the IRA and Bobby, for sure, on the Jamaicans, though I definitely can't send him after that bunch alone." And I can't send Cassie along with him, she thought. She's not ready for that kind of pressure. "Can I have Alice Long detailed to me for this job?"

He was nodding his acquiescence before she finished speaking, and adding, "But you're going to have to get Cassie Ali back on the books or let her go, Maglione. I can't carry her any longer. Now, what do you have on the back burner that she and the rest of your people can be working on?"

"Missing lesbians," she retorted.

He dropped a beat but recovered too quickly for her to enjoy his all too brief consternation. "Missing from where, for how long, and how come I'm just hearing about it? And what kind of missing? As in they got a new girlfriend and forgot to tell the old one, or missing as in nobody knows where they are?"

"You're just hearing about it because all I've got right now are rumors based on concerns. At least four women, all of them new to town, have disappeared without a trace within the last eighteen months or so. Because they were newcomers, they didn't have a solid circle of friends yet, just a few new acquaintances. But those acquaintances think it's more than a little odd that four people, all of them solid citizens with jobs and property, would just disappear without notice or a trace."

"And you think it's worth looking into?" He pressed her. She knew he'd respect her hunches because she'd earned that respect, but she also knew he wouldn't just turn her loose to pursue a wild goose chase.

"Yes, sir, I do." She recalled her conversation with Marianne, whom she'd known for twenty years. She'd been a bartender or owned a bar the entire time and she'd seen, heard, and done everything at least once, and she didn't panic or overreact ever. She was the kind of person whose intuitions could be trusted; and if Marianne felt there was something "mucho squirrelly" about the disappearance of the four women, then Gianna was prepared to accept that there could, indeed, be something worth looking into.

"Will your sources talk to the cops?"

She nodded, again impressed with his level of awareness. Not every victim of a hate crime, or every observer of one, trusted the police sufficiently to confide in them. Marianne would talk because she had nothing to hide and she feared no person or thing. "I'll put Cassie, Kenny and Linda on this," she said, hoping he heard and felt her contrition. He didn't deserve her pique. And just as she was deciding she owed him an apology, he put his foot down on her toe again.

"I know you can work both of these simultaneously, Maglione, and I expect you to. Along with the daily reports I'll expect." He picked up a folder from his desk and gave it to her. "This is the Irish file. What time do you want Detective Long to report to you tomorrow?"

What a crafty bastard he was! "Nine o'clock," she answered, crossing to the door and opening it.

"I'm counting on you, Maglione."

"Yes, sir," Gianna said, and closed the door behind her, relieved to be out of the glare of his scrutiny. No matter how long she worked for him, or how well she thought she knew him, he always managed either to surprise or annoy her. At the moment she was annoyed. He was constantly after her to behave

27

more like a lieutenant, which meant she should monitor and direct her cases from her office and not work her cases in the field with her subordinates, and she knew that he took heat for her past behavior: showing up at crime scenes in the middle of the night and punching out perps and spending the night on the couch in her office. Lieutenants weren't cops, they were paper-pushers, politicians-in-training, the future captains and deputy chiefs and assistant chiefs. His demand that she submit daily reports on the progress of both cases meant that he didn't want her in the field. He wanted her in the office, probably in uniform a couple of days a week. He'd clipped her wings and there was nothing she could do about it.

Mimi was releasing all her pent up anger and frustration on city editor Tyler Carson and he was allowing it, though it would serve no useful purpose, except perhaps to relieve Mimi of the weight of her fury. But it wouldn't change her situation because Tyler was not her editor. He was her friend and, in a pinch, her protector; and while he could— and often did— put in a good word to the higher-ups on her behalf or in her defense, he could not assign her to stories.

"Did you read this pile of shit?" Mimi brandished a copy of the Trimble lawsuit, then tossed it across the table at him. "Tell me why I should have to be put through this kind of mess."

"Comes with the territory. There've been a couple of those with my name on them." ˉHe picked up the document, glanced at it, and put it down.

"I'll quit, Tyler, I swear I will."

"I believe you, Patterson, but you'll be playing right into his sweaty little palms if you do that. The little weasel would like nothing better than for you to walk away."

Mimi knew he was right. "Weasel" Wassily, her editor and the head of the Special Projects Unit, was an Ivy League Neanderthal who, despite the dawning of the 21st century, hadn't yet accepted that women and Blacks had a legitimate place in the newsroom and who hated not only her presence, but the fact that Mimi was his brightest star. Tyler was right: he wouldn't, of his own volition, get rid of her; nor would he allow her to make a lateral move— say, to Carson's desk. But he'd accept her resignation in a heartbeat.

She put her elbows on the table and cradled her chin in her hands and glared balefully at Tyler, who was chewing a big bite of his club sandwich and reading a folded-up section of the *New York Times*, while taking cursory glances at a stack of summer intern applications. Mimi didn't mind. Tyler always did three things at the same time, though the activity usually involved talking on two telephones while editing copy. But since they were at lunch and not in the office, he made do with what was at hand. She took a bite of her veggie burger and grabbed the section of the New York paper that Tyler wasn't reading, and they ate and read in silence for a while until Mimi saw an article by someone she knew.

"Look at this! I know this guy! He covered the state legislature for years, and now he's doing sports. So why can't I switch to the arts and entertainment desk, Tyler?"

"I'm not the one who won't let you, Patterson."

"No, but you *are* the one who agreed that a 'certain expertise' was required to cover the arts." Mimi still was pissed at what she considered his betrayal.

He put down his sandwich and the paper, wiped his mouth on his napkin, and looked at her, green eyes serious behind the rims of his tortoise shell glasses. "But it's the truth, Patterson, and you know it. Everything is much more complicated than it used to be. You've gotta know something about film to cover it. You've gotta know something about theater and music to cover them. It's not enough any more just to be interested in a subject. You can't cover what that new artistic director is doing any more than the theater critic can cover government graft and corruption."

"And I can't cover it any more. I truly wouldn't care if

every bureaucrat in every government in D.C., Maryland and Virginia stole every penny from every treasury and they all came tumbling down. Not only wouldn't I want to write about it, I wouldn't even want to read about it." And what she felt when she said those words let her know that she truly needed a break from her routine, or she really would quit the job that she had loved for so long. She saw that Tyler knew it, too.

"Why don't you get away from here for a while? You've got plenty of vacation time. A couple of weeks in the mountains or on the beach and you'll feel differently about things. And maybe by the time you get back the stupid lawsuit will have returned to the fairyland where it originated."

"That's what Gianna said."

"How is your gorgeous police person?"

The one topic that could divert Mimi's attention from her work, and Tyler's signal that he'd rather they spent their rare time out of the office being friends instead of colleagues. He'd told her he was gay when they worked a story together a year and a half earlier that involved the murders of half a dozen closeted, married, and wealthy gay professionals. One of the victims had been a friend of Tyler's closeted, married FBI-agent boyfriend, and Gianna had been the targeted sixth victim...targeted because her previous lover was a closeted, married woman. Mimi still shuddered at the thought of Gianna held captive and beaten by the madwoman released from a mental institution because she no longer was "a danger to herself or to others." "She'll be fine if the department doesn't shut down the Hate Crimes Unit and stick her behind a desk, shuffling papers. Then we'd both be unemployed."

Mid-chew, Tyler switched from caring friend back to canny newspaper editor again. "Are you serious?"

"Gianna's seriously worried it could happen."

"That would be an incredibly stupid thing to do. You should write about it, Mimi."

"Are you crazy?" Mimi had raised her voice before she

could stop herself, and now she looked self-consciously around the restaurant. Several of the closest diners were kindly pretending that her outburst hadn't occurred. For almost the entirety of their relatively brief relationship, Mimi and Gianna had clashed over the extent to which their work got in the way of their lives. For Mimi to write about a confidence so rarely revealed would probably spell the end of them.

Tyler grinned an apology. He had first hand experience with their personal life versus business life conflict. "I guess that's not such a good idea, although it is a great story. I could assign it to that new reporter, the one from Albuquerque. He's a really good writer."

"No, Tyler, you could not do that. And why couldn't you? Because the only way you could know about any talk of disbanding the Hate Crimes Unit would be through me. So, unless you want to see me nailed to a cross in Judiciary Square, you'll forget I said anything. Unless, of course, you can develop an independent source, say, in the Chief's office. Then it wouldn't have anything to do with me."

"You're incorrigible, Patterson."

"That's why I'm so good at my job."

"Yeah, it is. And speaking of which, what are you going to do about that?"

Mimi shrugged, sighed, and shook her head. She didn't know what she was going to do about her job or her current feelings about her job, or her feeling that she'd been betrayed by her boss and the company attorneys. "Maybe I will get away for a while. I'll lie in the sun and read books. I don't remember the last time I read a book all the way through."

Tyler leaned across the table and peered at her. "How do you read a book, Patterson, if not all the way through?"

She laughed. "Three or four pages, five at the most, before I fall asleep. Then I have to read those same three or four or five pages the next night because I don't remember what I read the night before. Takes me ages to finish anything," she said, warming to the thought of spending a week or so sleeping and reading in the sun. Then she thought again about the reason she was even considering a vacation this time of year, and the warm feeling evaporated. "I better go tell the Weasel before I change my mind."

"*Ask* him, Patterson. You *ask* your editor for permission to take the time off, you don't *tell* him. Especially that one."

Mimi crossed her right knee over the left one but otherwise didn't move or speak. She watched her editor across the desk, wishing that she were British and living in that time when there would have been more appropriate language for conversation with him. What she wanted to do was to tell him to go fuck himself; to call him a spineless, dickless wonder; to tell him he was a jerk and an incompetent asshole. What would Dorothy L. Sayers or P.D. James say to him? Or Zora Neale Hurston, for that matter? What was a toady?

"Don't be such a frog."

He blushed and sputtered. She'd insulted him and he knew it, but she hadn't profaned or disrespected him, and since she hadn't actually called him a name, he couldn't really take offense. "Why do you find it necessary to be so unpleasant?"

"*I'm* unpleasant? You go out of your way to make my life miserable and *I'm* unpleasant? You block every effort I make to search out good stories. You block any attempt I make to work with other editors, which I do because you so clearly don't want me working for you. You hang me out to dry in this Trimble business when you know full well that I am not at fault. And now, knowing that I'm in a shit position *because* you and your lawyer pals hung me out to dry, you want to prevent me from taking some time off. Why don't you just fire me, Wea...ah...Wassily. Isn't that what people like you do to people like me?"

He leaned back in his chair, as if the expanse of his desk weren't sufficient distance between them. "Would you care to explain that?"

Mimi leaned forward in her chair. "I'm sure I don't need to explain the concept of power to you." She stood up. "I'm taking some time off, a week or so, beginning, oh, say, Friday. I'll put the request in writing, like I'm supposed to. And if you deny the request, I'll expect a reason in writing. Like you're supposed to." She was half way out the door when a thought turned her around. "Trimble's wife's lawsuit is frivolous. Isn't there a law against that?"

"Tyler's right, Mimi, you don't tell your boss what you're going to do."

"Spoken like a true boss, Lieutenant Maglione, Ma'am. But you didn't answer my question."

Gianna pushed a gust of air through pursed lips and shook her head. "I can't get away right now, Mimi, for even a day, to say nothing of a week. The chief walked all over me this morning, wearing combat boots it felt like. This is probably the last time I'll be off this early until Christmas, so enjoy it while you can."

They were having drinks and dinner at *The Bayou*, where the excitement of the weekend's grand opening party lingered. They'd had to sit at the bar until a table in the restaurant became available. And now, all the bar stools were occupied and the dance floor was filling and it was not yet nine o'clock on a Monday night.

"What'd the chief do--"

"Hi, Pretty Lady. Can I get you a refill?" The bartender, tall, blond and leering, leaned in toward Gianna, resting her elbows on the bar and cutting off Mimi's access. "And wouldn't you like something with a little more punch than cranberry juice? I could splash a little vodka into that juice, what do ya think?" She grinned and winked. Gianna hadn't moved or spoken.

"I think you should go splash vodka for somebody who asks for it," Mimi said. "We were talking. You interrupted."

The bartender stood up straight and looked at Mimi. Her pale blue eyes narrowed and she licked her lips. "I wasn't talking to you."

"And neither of us was talking to you. We were talking to each other. And we're both old enough to know how to order drinks, so we'll call you if we need you."

Before the bartender could reply Marianne was behind them. "Your table's ready and you'd better hurry because the line is growing. And did I mention that you'll have to eat fast?" She looked like a Swedish movie star with her long, straight blonde hair framing her face and her kohl-lined blue eyes. And then there was the way she enhanced the scarlet tee shirt with its *Bayou* logo.

They stood up and Mimi reached into her pocket for money to pay for their drinks. Marianne waved it off. "On the house, Trudi. If I know these two, it's nothing but juice or club soda anyway. Besides which, they'll pay dearly when I get 'em into the restaurant." Marianne rubbed her hands together gleefully, laughed wickedly, and led them past the crowded dance floor into the restaurant and to their table. The place was as packed as it had been on Friday night.

"This is amazing," Mimi said, surveying the crowd. "I love this!"

"Mimi, I thought you were blowing smoke when you said you'd become a regular, but damn if you're not making good on your word."

Mimi laid her right hand across her chest. "I am a woman of my word, if nothing else."

"And you've been a few other things in your time, the way I hear it," Marianne said in a tone of voice that made Mimi wince. Jesus! How long did a reputation follow a person? And she hadn't even known Marianne back then.

Gianna raised her eyebrows. "You'll have to tell me all about that, Mare. Some other time, though, when we can talk alone." Then, to Mimi's overwhelming relief, she changed the subject. "Do you have a menu I can take with me? I'm treating my team to a working dinner tomorrow night, and since they're not going to like what I have to say, I thought plying them with good food would make the bad news easier to take."

"What aren't they going to like?" Mimi asked as Marianne left to get the menu, hoping to keep Gianna away from a discussion of her past reputation, which she didn't even want to think about, to say nothing of discuss, especially with Gianna. She need not have worried. Her checkered reputation was the farthest thing from Gianna's mind.

"Tell me exactly what Cassandra Ali said to you the other night," she said. "Tell me what she said and how she said it and how she seemed to you."

And as Mimi brought the image of Cassandra Ali into focus, she was wondering what was serious enough that Gianna would risk bringing the young cop back to work when she'd just said that she wasn't ready.

CHAPTER THREE

Not even abundant good food succeeded in lifting the spirits of the Hate Crimes team, though the presence of Cassandra Ali brought smiles all around. Hesitant, tentative smiles, since Cassie's return was provisional; Gianna had made that fact quite clear. Cassie wanted to be back and Gianna, against her better judgment, was willing to allow the young officer to test herself. She'd had Cassie come in early so she could prepare her for the news that Alice Long would be detailed to the Unit to work with Bobby. They all knew Alice; she and Tony Watkins, both seasoned undercover cops, had worked a case with them several months ago. But what they didn't know was that Alice had requested permanent assignment to Hate Crimes if Cassie's injuries prevented her return, or that Alice was a lesbian and that she certainly would be Gianna's choice to replace Cassie should that become necessary. Gianna watched Cassie closely as she processed what she was being told: Her return was provisional; her schedule was limited; another cop was being brought in to what would have been her job.

She nodded her acceptance. "I'm just glad to be back, Boss, and I'll do whatever you say." And Gianna knew she would.

But none of them would so readily or easily embrace the news that they were to be split up for their next assignment, and they were absolutely livid that the split was to be along racial lines. Here they were, the Hate Crimes Unit, and only the white members could work the Irish angle of the case and only the Black members could work the Jamaican angle.

"Well, since I'm Black Irish, how about I become the swing member of the team?" Tim McCreedy was so upset and angry that he could find no energy for his "queen routine," when he collapsed his six foot-plus weight lifter's body into a prancing, mincing stereotype of a screaming queen.

"I know how you feel," Gianna said, standing and walking to the end of the table where they all sat, so that she could make eye contact with each of them. "I share your feelings. But we've no choice in the matter. The assignment wasn't a request, it was an order, and we follow orders. The smart thing would be to do it quickly and efficiently--"

"If the IRA could be found quickly and efficiently, there wouldn't have been four hundred years of bloodshed over there," Tim said, still nasty and snarly, but he withered under the look he got from Gianna, and mumbled a "Sorry, Boss."

"What I meant," Gianna continued equably, "was that we accept and embrace our new assignments quickly and efficiently — and graciously. Without rancor. Let's not waste time and energy being angry. Let's find the guns so we can get on with our other duties."

"But why us?" asked Kenny Chang in a tone of voice that was, for him, borderline belligerent. "Isn't that a job for the Feds?"

"It's a job for us if we're ordered to do it," Gianna replied curtly.

"Are we about to get shit-canned?" asked Bobby Gilliam, cracking his knuckles, a very recent and extremely annoying habit. "'Cause if we are, I think that sucks! No other unit in the Department can match our case clearance rate--"

"Enough, Bobby! Where do you get this stuff? I need your minds on the job at hand."

"That's all everybody's talking about, Boss. We were hoping you could clear things up for us." Linda Lopez was trying for "the voice of reason" tone, but the words came out a lament. "We're a team. If something's going to happen to us, we should know. All of us."

"I have no idea what you mean. What exactly is it that everybody's talking about and what does it have to do with us?"

"The budget cuts," Bobby said. The word is that the City

Council budget committee is swinging a wide axe and heads are rolling all over town," Bobby said.

"Well, our heads are still on," Gianna snapped with more authority than she felt. Was that why the Chief handed her such a monster of a case? So she could prove her worth and guarantee her continued existence? "And I need the brains inside your heads focused on the task at hand."

"The task being to look for a bunch of Irish assholes with a cache of automatic weapons," Tim said in a very reasonable, calm tone of voice, which also was borderline belligerent.

"And being that you *are* an Irish asshole, McCreedy," Cassie retorted, sounding almost like her old self, "that should be a piece of cake for you." She and Tim were best friends, and her return to self returned him to self and he loosened his body and dropped his wrist and tilted his head in her direction; and while he didn't speak, everybody heard what he would have said and the tension in the room evaporated. The air lightened, bodies relaxed, Bobby and Eric scooped more food onto their plates, and Linda opened another soda.

"So, Boss, since we know what the white guys are doing, what's the job for the queers and the Negroes?" Cassie asked.

Gianna stifled a gasp; she'd been too long without Cassie's very politically incorrect tendencies. But before she could respond, Kenny Chang, sounding wounded, offered that he wasn't queer or a Negro.

"For purposes of this assignment, Kenny, my brother, all those who ain't white and Irish, are queers or Negroes," Cassie intoned.

The laughter and cat-calls that greeted this pronouncement were an even bigger release of tension than before, and Gianna let them go for another few moments, so relieved was she at their return to the irreverent, spirited, cynical, intelligent bantering that was their hallmark and which endeared them to her. She joined in the laughter, ate two more spiced shrimp and drank another glass of ginger beer, before restoring order. "All right, gentle persons of all persuasions, lend me your ears." And as quickly as the silliness had descended, order prevailed, and Gianna outlined in detail what the chief had told her, and then she told them what Marianne had told her.

"That's it?" Cassie asked incredulously. "That's all we've got to go on?"

"That's it," Gianna said, "but if there's something there, it's enough. Kenny and Linda, you two start with female deaths in the forty-to-sixty age range, everything but natural causes, concentrating on Jane Does and out-of-towners and going back eighteen months...no, make it twenty-four. Cassie, you begin at *The Bayou* and spread out to every woman's bar in the region. Talk to the bartenders and owners--"

Kenny interrupted. "Are they the only ones who get to go to *The Bayou?*"

"Let me be sure I understand: You're *not* a Negro but you *are* a lesbian? Bit confused, are you, Dearie?" Tim was at full-tilt queen.

"I only meant," Kenny finally managed, when he could stop laughing long enough to explain himself, "that I want to be where that food is. Do they let men in? Will they let me in?"

Cassie got up and walked around the table to Kenny and hugged his head. "They let in Negroes and queers, so you'll be all right. Just stick with me, pal."

"How're we going to know who's lesbian?" Linda asked into the moment of silence that followed the silliness, and nobody was on the same page with her. "The Jane Does, the out-of-towners, the DBs," she explained. "They don't have red *"Ls"* glued on them. How're we gonna know?"

"Concentrate on women in the target age range, and on any dead body that wasn't claimed immediately. Use your noses, people, we're playing hunches here, and in the final analysis, there may be nothing to find. But if there is, we're going to find it."

"Boss?" Bobby spoke quietly and a bit hesitantly and Gianna knew what he was going to say.

"What is it, Bobby?"

"I like Alice Long just fine. She's a damn good cop. But if Cassie's ready to be back on the job, then why can't she work the case with me?"

"Good question, Bobby. And the answer is that Cassie *isn't* ready to be back on the job. Her return is provisional, and she understands that, and I thought you all did, too." Gianna gave Cassie a steady look and the young cop nodded. "She's working a light schedule and I'll be keeping a very close watch on her." Gianna stood up. "Whoever's taking food home, wrap it up. Don't leave anything in here."

The Think Tank, home of the Hate Crimes Unit, in its former life was a small conference room directly below Gianna's office. Newly furnished— "new" being a relative term— it held four wooden desks and two metal ones, one conference table, two new four-drawer file cabinets that actually locked, two new computers that actually functioned more often that not, a television and a VCR, and a paper shredder. A blackboard ran the length of one wall, and a projection screen hung on the adjacent wall. And, since the arrival of the new furnishings, there were mice. Nobody had seen them, though they left evidence of their existence. And they ate any and everything, making it impossible to leave a candy bar or a bag of chips in a desk drawer. And since not a single one of them professed to be willing or able to deal with a trap with a mouse caught in it, their only recourse was to try and starve the critters into taking up residence elsewhere.

"Eric, you and Tim, my office, eight thirty tomorrow morning. Bobby, I'll see you and Alice at nine. The rest of you report here every day at four thirty. Cassie, I need to see you before you leave."

The clean-up and leave-taking proceeded rapidly, and Gianna and Cassie faced each other across the table in the empty and quiet room.

"I know you don't think I'm ready to be back," Cassie said quickly, preempting her boss, "and I really and truly do

40

appreciate the chance to show you differently."

Gianna held the young cop's gaze. If ever she were forced to admit having a favorite, she'd name Cassandra Ali. She was smart, aggressive, fearless, instinctive, loyal, and hard-headed: a dangerous combination of worthy traits. "I'm not comfortable with it, Cassie, and I'm worried that in trying to prove something to me, you'll hurt yourself."

"So, why bring me back?" But even as she asked the question, the answer dawned on her face. "It was that or lose me forever? The budget cuts are real?"

Gianna had known that Cassie would figure out the truth, but that didn't make her admission any easier. She nodded, keeping a tight lock on Cassie's gaze.

"I'm grateful that you think enough of me to take that kind of risk, Boss."

"You're a good cop, Cassie."

A hint of a smile lifted the left corner of Cassie's mouth. "That's what your girlfriend said." And the smile increased at Gianna's wary surprise and Cassie quickly and wisely changed the subject. "I really am doing all right, Boss."

"All right isn't good enough. You're blowing off the shrink. And don't look so surprised. Of course I talk to her. It's only on her recommendation that I'd ever agree to take you back into the Unit. And that's why your return is 'provisional.' Until she's convinced that you're ready, I won't be convinced that you're ready."

Cassie shook her head angrily. "I would have been fine if they'd let me see the therapist of my choice."

"It doesn't work that way. Not very many therapists are qualified to assess the fitness of police officers for duty, and you know that, Cassie."

"But Dr. Connors is a wonderful therapist!" Cassie wailed, sounding more like the injured 25-year old that she was than like a hardened cop she aspired to be, and having no idea that her boss knew exactly how wonderful Beverly Connors was. Not only were

41

they good friends, but Beverly was Mimi's former lover.

"You can see Dr. Connors on your own time, and I think it's probably a good idea if you do. But you're also going to have to keep regular appointments with the Department therapist, Cassie, and she's going to have to be able make an unequivocal recommendation for your return. Am I clear?" Gianna stood to indicate that the discussion was over.

"Yes, Boss," Cassie said in a small voice, and she, too, stood up. "And I really do appreciate you taking a chance on me."

Gianna walked over to the young woman and touched her shoulder. "The risk is all yours, Cassie. If I'm making a mistake bringing you back before you're ready, you're the one who gets hurt. I'm being selfish."

And instantly uncomfortable with the stark truth of her words, Gianna crossed to the door, opened it, waited for Cassie to exit ahead of her, and turned off the light, giving no thought to the nocturnal activities of mice, and wishing instead that she could go home and be with Mimi instead of upstairs to her office to finish her monthly report, due on the chief's desk in fourteen hours.

Mimi sat in her car across the street from *The Bayou*, deciding whether to go in. Being a regular was one thing; being predictable was something else entirely. Yet, she found that she didn't know what to when she didn't work twelve and thirteen-hour days. She'd already been to the gym and had a workout and a sauna, and now she was ravenous. So, why not eat where she enjoyed the food and the atmosphere? Better still, why not just resume the habit of working all the time and relieve herself of having to wrestle with such mundane matters?

Annoyed with herself for her mental ramblings, she was about to drive off when she saw Cassandra Ali walk in the front door, and there was something about the way she carried herself that captured Mimi's interest. She knew that Gianna had met with the Unit that night, and that she'd fed them *Bayou* food. So, what was Cassie Ali doing here? A date? The comfort of a friendly crowd? Mimi was out of the car and sprinting across the street before she allowed herself time to wonder what the hell she was doing, or why.

She got inside the front door in time to see Cassie climb up on a bar stool. The dance floor was packed but only half the bar stools were occupied and Marianne walked immediately over to her. Mimi slid sideways, out of Marianne's sight line, and angled around toward the rear of the bar and snuggled against one of the floor-to-ceiling beams that gave the place its rustic, on-the- water look and feel. She saw Cassie reach into her pocket, take out her badge, and place it on the counter in front of her, so that only Marianne could see it. She smiled, extended her hand to Cassie, and picked up a telephone from somewhere beneath the counter. She punched some buttons, waited, spoke briefly, and returned the phone to its hiding place. She and Cassie talked for a few seconds before the tall, lean, blonde— and rude— bartender named Trudi replaced her, and Cassie followed Marianne toward the kitchen and, Mimi knew, Marianne's office in the corridor behind the kitchen and storage area.

"Well looky there," she muttered, secretly pleased that her assessment of Gianna and Marianne's intense conversation the night of the party was on the mark. Obviously there was something serious on Marianne's mind— serious enough to require police attention, and serious enough for her to discuss it with Gianna in the middle of a party. But what? Something to do with the club? Mimi thought not. The place had just opened; and anyway, Gianna wouldn't send a Hate Crimes cop to investigate anything but a hate crime. She was a by-the-book cop through and through. So, Mimi mused, a hate crime either had occurred or Marianne was afraid that one would, meaning that perhaps it was about the bar after all. Perhaps neighbors in the upscale, trendy neighborhood objected to the presence of a lesbian establishment. But that didn't make sense, either. Gay bars and clubs on Capitol Hill were nothing new, and Mimi knew that in the 1970's there were almost a dozen gay bars and clubs and restaurants and book stores in this neighborhood. But that was then and this was now.

Renee, Marianne's partner in life and business, emerged from the game room and looked immediately toward the bar, expecting to see Marianne. She frowned at the presence of the substitute bartender and started toward the bar. Mimi hurried to cut her off, formulating a plan in her mind.

"Hey, Mimi! I ordered that bar stool with your name on it, but I'm thinking now I should have measured your butt to guarantee a perfect fit."

Renee was slightly taller than Mimi's five-foot-seven, and with her silver-streaked black hair and Mediterranean coloring, she was as dark as Marianne was fair.

Mimi took her ribbing with good grace and admitted that she'd had no idea what she was missing by being such a workaholic. "But it's no fun being normal alone. Gianna's still working like a fiend. In fact, one of her Unit is holed up with Marianne now." She watched the look of understanding that crossed Renee's face. "So, should I blame you or Marianne if Gianna spends tonight with Officer Ali instead of with me?"

Renee raised her hands, palms forward, in a defensive gesture. "It wasn't my idea, and I couldn't talk Marianne out of it. You know how she is when she gets a hold of some idea or thought or feeling." Renee shook her head in resignation.

Mimi commiserated. "Yeah. A lot like Gianna."

"But there's nothing *there*," Renee said, sounding truly annoyed. "All Mare has to go on is some women who don't come into the bar anymore. *She* claims they've disappeared, but in reality, all she can say for a fact is that they've stopped coming to the bar. Which, last time I looked, they had a right to do, no matter how wonderful Mare is. And she's pretty wonderful, if I do say so myself."

Mimi's antennae were at attention. She worked hard at trying to sound both reasonable and sympathetic instead of on the scent of a story, while not seeming to discount Renee's assessment of her partner. "Come on, Renee. You know Marianne better than that. She's not a sky is falling kinda gal, so she must have some reason for believing that the women have disappeared."

"Oh, she's got reasons all right, and they all stink! Listen to this, Mimi: all these women were from out of town and they'd just moved to the D.C. area, OK?"

Mimi creased her brow and nodded to indicate that she was following the conversation, though internally she was screaming for Renee to get to the point.

"And these newcomers had claimed Marianne and the bar as family and home. You know how she is about family and home and creating a homey atmosphere in the bar. Two or three times a week, every week, these women were in the bar. One of 'em, a woman from somewhere in Georgia, I believe, even wanted to invest with us when she found out we were looking for larger space." Renee paused in her recitation and her face became serious. "She was the first one to stop coming in. That was more than a year ago and I have to admit, that one was pretty strange." The smile lines around her large, grey eyes crinkled and she pursed her lips.

"Strange how?" Mimi pounced on the information cat-like. "And why? Maybe she didn't like here and just moved back to Georgia."

Renee shook her head and the silver strands danced in the light. "She'd never have done that. She had just barely escaped one of those fanatical religious families. They'd actually kept this woman locked in an attic because she was a lesbian, and had some kind of preacher praying over her, in tongues, no less. Can you imagine? They wouldn't let her work, and they put her through an exorcism or some such bullshit, trying to get the devil out of her. No way she went back to that. And she loved it here. She had a condo out in Reston, on the lake."

"Condos on the lake in Reston don't come cheap," Mimi said, then stopped at the evil grin spreading across Renee's face

45

and waited for the details.

"That's the other reason she wouldn't go back down south. Her folks might have been religious crazies, but they were rich religious crazies. She stole half a million dollars from them when she left."

"Half a million dollars!" Mimi yelped. "Hell, I'd disappear, too, if I'd stolen that much money from somebody I was related to. Disappear is the least she could do." Mimi knew her cynicism was riding on the surface, so she tried to tone it down; after all, the woman wasn't a government official stealing from the public coffers. She was just an abused woman stealing from her abusive family. "Maybe she was overcome with guilt and joined a convent."

"Believe me, Millicent Cartcher didn't join *anything* with a religious aspect to it. She just dropped off the radar screen. Not a blip anywhere." Renee shook her head, and again the silver strands danced in the light.

Mimi's interest had waned and unless Marianne had told Gianna more than Renee had told her, Mimi couldn't imagine what there was to investigate. "Well, good thing Gianna's the cop and not me, because I can't make anything out of that."

"Me, either," Renee said. "I think Marianne's got Gianna sniffing around the wrong bush. Just as long as she doesn't waste too much of the tax payers' money while she's at it," she said, and then quickly apologized as she misread the look on Mimi's face. "I didn't mean that Gianna wastes taxpayers' money."

"The money," Mimi said, instincts on alert again. "What happened to the money?"

"What money?"

"Millicent whoever's money. The half million dollars and the condo on the lake. If she wasn't in contact with her real family, and if you and Marianne and women in the bar were her only other 'family,' what happened to the money? And the condo? Does Marianne know?"

Renee's face wrinkled in a thoughtful, puzzled frown. "I

46

don't know. We called a couple of times after she stopped coming in and as I recall, we got her answering machine once, and then one of those 'that number has been disconnected' messages."

But Mimi was no longer listening. She was thinking about the money. Even with the cash purchase of a condo, there could have been as much as a hundred thousand dollars left, more if the woman had a job earning decent money. "What kind of work did she do, Renee? Do you know?"

"Sure. She was a veterinarian. Made house calls, so grateful was she not to be looking after farm animals. She said cats and dogs and birds were a breeze after pigs and cows and horses. That's why we're not the only ones lamenting her absence. Every dyke and queen in a thirty mile radius with more than one cat misses Millie."

Now Mimi was interested, and when she probed her internal responses to learn why, the answer depressed her: The story— she already was calling it that— had all the elements of one of her governmental graft and corruption stories. Where, she asked herself, was the human interest element? Couldn't she just care about a story because she cared about the people involved? Because a woman was missing? Not because half a million dollars was missing? Maybe that's what Tyler and the other editors knew about her that she didn't know about herself: that she couldn't cover entertainment and the arts because she couldn't find the soft underbelly of a story, the humanity of a story.

"What are you thinking?" Renee asked.

"That I need to go home and go to bed," Mimi replied. "Tell Mare I'm sorry I missed seeing her." And she turned and walked out of the bar, immediately missing its warmth and the good smells. She crossed the street against the light, climbed into her car, and drove home, the recent self-discovery a stronger feeling within her than the gnawing hunger pains. She was at home, in panties and bra, staring into the open refrigerator, when she remembered that she was supposed to be at Gianna's tonight. And for a moment, she contemplated dressing and driving the

47

ten minutes to Gianna's place. The moment passed. She was too committed to exploring what was happening inside her.

She recalled both Gianna and Beverly making cracks about her lack of humanity, and she wondered, now, whether they really were teasing her, or whether real concern lurked beneath their words. She could hear Beverly's voice: *"Don't tell me you're becoming a human being."* The comment had stung at the time, Mimi recalled, even as she'd convinced herself that Bev was joking. Only Bev didn't joke about that kind of thing. She'd been a school counselor for years until completing her Ph.D. and going into private practice with several other therapists. People's feelings always had been important to Bev; and Mimi's lack of regard for other people's feelings— especially Bev's— had been a major cause of their break-up.

"So, Patterson, you're a selfish, insensitive, uncaring, unfeeling jerk," she said to the food inside the refrigerator.

The refrigerator hummed loudly, as if suggesting that she either get something from it or close the door. She grabbed a bottle of seltzer water from the top shelf and slammed the refrigerator door shut. She got a can of nuts from the cabinet, and went to bed.

CHAPTER FOUR

The mood in the Think Tank that afternoon was, if not buoyant, at least more energetic than it had been in months, though there still was some residual grumbling about the split in their assignments. But Alice Long had been welcomed back warmly and she was a good fit. She and Bobby were comfortable with each other, as were she and Cassie.

"Eric and Tim, let's hear from you first." Gianna, clad in black jeans and Western boots, her shoulder holster visible under her left arm since her jacket was upstairs in her office, leaned back in her chair and propped her feet on the table.

Eric scowled, curling his lips in distaste. "What's that line about mad dogs and Irishmen?"

Alice Long guffawed. "It was 'Englishmen,' and it said that only mad dogs and Englishmen were crazy enough to go outside during the hottest part of the day in India and Africa and the Caribbean— all those places where the British had colonies. It was the native's way of calling the English stupid." She was still laughing when Eric, face as red as his hair, recovered enough to speak.

"Anyway, we hung out most of the day at that pub where these gun runners are supposed to hang out, and I gotta tell you, Boss, there wasn't a guy in that room who could hatch a plot to send flowers to a funeral, to say nothing of buying illegal guns to ship illegally to Ireland."

Tim chimed in with a wide grin. "That's the truth, Boss. As much as I hate the all-Irish-are-drunks stereotype, every guy in there was a big time boozer, and I swear half of them were on the job, don't you think?" And he looked to Eric for confirmation, readily receiving it. "Nobody could seriously think of looking for gunrunners in the Shamrock," he concluded.

"Somebody could," Alice said quietly, and every eye turned to her. "Bobby and I paid a visit to the Eight Rivers Lounge on 14th Street. That's one of the main hang-outs for the Ganja crew..." She hesitated briefly at the sideways look Gianna gave her, then continued with her story.

Alice Long had worked undercover long enough to have acquired vast stores of knowledge on many different topics and Gianna knew it; knew better than to question or challenge it, though she hated having it sprung on her in the middle of an investigation.

"Anyway," Alice continued, "I went in there pretending I had to use the bathroom, and attracted a little attention."

She was stopped this time by the hoots of laughter. Alice Long was a stunner by anybody's definition, though the only time she ever traded on her physical attributes was to benefit her job.

"I'll bet you did attract attention, Honey Chile," Tim drawled from his queenly pose, imitating Alice's South Carolina Gulla accent. "You'd attract attention at a drag show, Miss Long, Girl, with your fine self."

Gianna had to rap on the table to restore order, and it took several minutes more to learn from Alice that the Eight Rivers, named for the city of Ocho Rios in Jamaica, was the field office of the head of the Northwest Ganja Crew. She frowned, questioning Alice's terminology, though not the veracity of her information.

"The Ganjas split a couple of months ago. You remember a shoot-out in a church parking lot on Rhode Island Avenue in the middle of a Monday afternoon?" Everyone did, and Alice continued. "That marked the split. The southeast Ganjas just want to sell their weed, which is some of the most expensive— and highest quality— on the East Coast, and keep a low profile. Their attitude is the cops don't mess with weed dealers if there's no violence. The northwest Ganjas want to control the drug trade in D.C., period, and they don't mind using violence. In fact, they like it, which is why the southeast crew doesn't want any part of them. The northwest crew has battled the Russians, the Colombians— anybody white, who's dealing in D.C."

"Hold it!" Kenny Chang stood up. "You're saying that there's a gang that deals drugs based on racial pride?"

Alice shook her head and made a thumbs down gesture with her right hand. "There ain't no pride involved, Kenny, just your below average, run-of-the-mill, mean, greedy, drug-dealin' scumbags."

"Is there an Irish drug cartel?" Cassie asked. "Is that why the Ganjas are so focused on stealing their guns?"

"Nope," Alice said, shaking her head. "Not that I've ever heard. They want the guns from the Irish 'cause the Irish are the ones who'll have the guns, all boxed up nice and neat. No politics or pride involved."

"I need to know how you know all this, Alice, and you can tell me privately if necessary," Gianna said.

"Just so it doesn't leave this room, I'll tell you," Alice said.

"It won't leave this room," Gianna responded, not needing to check for a consensus, though there was one as heads nodded around the table.

"I just completed a two-month undercover assignment on the drug task force. Intelligence gathering. Longest two months of my life, and that's the truth."

Gianna could believe it, given the sense of dread she heard in Alice's voice; but what she was feeling was renewed anger at the chief. No wonder he had so readily agreed to Alice Long's assignment; he'd probably have assigned her himself if Gianna hadn't asked for her. Crafty bastard! She said, "So you agree that we'd better find the guns before the Ganjas find them."

"Oh hell, yes!" Alice said with feeling. "What Tim and Detective Ashby saw at the Shamrock today might have been just some harmless old drunks, but those Irish guys with the guns are anything but. I heard the Ganjas talking about 'em, and the last thing you want is a gunfight between those two groups."

51

Gianna locked eyes with Eric, remembering the Chief's analogy of the two elephants doing battle, and he nodded his understanding of her message: Find the damn guns before the Ganjas find them. Then she turned her attention to Cassie, Linda and Kenny. She wasn't surprised that Cassie already had started work on the case; Marianne had called earlier to thank her for taking seriously the matter of the missing women. But she was surprised at how Linda and Kenny reacted to Cassie's actions. Even though they'd had all day to smooth their ruffled feathers, they still were annoyed at Cassie's trip to *The Bayou* the previous night. And, Gianna could see, Cassie regretted having done anything to irritate her colleagues. "I'm sorry, guys, I really am. I was just so glad to be back on the job and to have something to do."

"But suppose something had happened!" Kenny finally exploded, releasing not anger but fearful concern, totally confusing Cassie.

"Something like what?"

"Like...like...anything! I don't know like what, Cassie! Like you needed back-up and you were in there by yourself and nobody knew you were there."

Cassie finally got it. "Oh, Geez, Kenny, I'm sorry. I wasn't thinking."

"Which is exactly why you shouldn't run off by yourself," Linda added in as snappish a tone as she'd ever used with any of them. "We're supposed to be a team."

"All right, you guys, I think she's got the message. Let's move on. You want to tell what you learned last night, Cassie?" Gianna thought she'd better get her talking before she burst into tears.

"I think what Kenny and Linda got from the ME is more important than what I got from the bar," Cassie offered, catching everybody by surprise.

"You've got something from the ME already?" Gianna hadn't expected anything useful from the medical examiner's officer for at least a week. Not only was the staff there overworked, it was overburdened by an archaic filing system, and by notoriously sloppy record-keeping by the police department which in turn, often rendered their own records suspect.

Their pique with Cassie finally put aside, Kenny and Linda looked more excited than any Hate Crimes cop had looked in months. "You know what a bas--"

"Grouch," Linda inserted.

"--grouch Dr. Shehee can be," Kenny said, referring to the legendarily grouchy bastard, Asa Sheehee, the chief medical examiner for the District of Columbia. "Well, we were expecting him to tear into us when we told him what we were after."

"But he smiled at us!" Linda chirped. "He actually smiled, and grabbed us by the arms and pulled us into his office. He grabbed this folder that was on top of this huge pile of sh--"

"Crap," Kenny said with a gotcha grin at Linda.

"--crap. Then he says we'll have to wait for anything going back as far as eighteen months or two years, but that we should take a look at the file on the Jane Doe from the other night."

"The other night!" Gianna and Eric spoke in unison, and listened with growing dismay as Kenny and Linda spilled out the details. The victim was an unidentified white female between forty and fifty years of age, discovered on the grounds of the Lincoln Memorial, her esophagus severed by a length of piano wire still embedded in her throat. She was expensively though conservatively dressed and Dr. Shehee speculated that her entire wardrobe, down to and including underwear, was brand new. No identification was found with or near the body, and the body bore no identifying marks. Except--"

"Except what?" Gianna demanded.

Kenny and Linda shared a look. "An intact hymen," Linda said quietly.

"A *what?*" Eric asked.

"A hymen," Kenny said. "That's the membrane--"

"I know *what* it is," Eric snapped. "I'm asking why Asa Shehee is making such a big deal out of a biological given. Every woman has one."

"But you won't find many heterosexual fifty-something year old women with one intact ," Gianna said quietly. "We need a photo of this woman..."

"It'll be ready tomorrow by noon," Linda said.

"Do you want us to show it to the owner at *The Bayou* to see if she recognizes her, or do you want to do that, Boss?" Kenny asked, knowing as they all did how deeply she involved herself in their cases. But the chief's dictum rang in her ears and she shook her head. She was to stick close to the office and behave like a lieutenant.

"If Marianne recognizes her, call me immediately. Then show that photo in every woman's bar between Richmond and Baltimore. The three of you decide how to divvy up the turf. I'm going to pay Dr. Shehee a visit, see if I can't help him make some sense out of his case files." The chief wouldn't object to her paying a visit to the ME. "Or I'll threaten to send Tim to do it..."

Tim McCreedy had displayed a talent for making sense out of the unholy mess that were departmental case files. And though an enormous effort had been made to improve both the system and the cops who functioned within it, sloppy files more often than not were the order of the day. And Tim McCreedy, despite all the odds against him, somehow managed to create order out of mayhem, earning him the enmity of those cops whose files needed fixing; and not because they begrudged him his successes, but because he always was at his queenly best whenever on such assignments. And it always happened that some macho cop took offense at Tim's behavior. The last one who called McCreedy a faggot took his meals through a straw for two months, and ate soft foods for another two. He bowed toward her. "Your wish is my command, your lieutenantness."

"Find those guns," she commanded. But her mind wasn't on guns. She was thinking about a Jane Doe with an intact hymen. Not proof, certainly, that the woman was a lesbian—penetration was an integral part of pleasurable sexual activity for many lesbians— but she had a feeling that Marianne would recognize the woman. She had a feeling that this Jane Doe and her intact hymen presented just the tip of something very deep and very ugly.

Mimi leaned back in her chair, propped her feet on the corner of the desk, and stared at the blinking cursor on her computer screen. She had been hung up on three times in the past seven minutes. Good thing she wasn't thin-skinned, she thought as she picked up the phone to call the next number on her list. Given the amount of rejection she received during the course of a normal work day, she'd make a good actor. She'd always heard that the first step toward becoming a successful actor was the ability to handle rejection. She punched in the numbers and counted the rings. More than four without an answer and she expected an answering machine, unless it was the home of somebody over the age of seventy; septuagenarians didn't rely heavily on modern technology. She wasn't even aware that this was knowledge she possessed; it was more a conclusion borne of habit. She spent half her life on the telephone— talking on it or waiting to talk to somebody on it or being disconnected from it.

She hung up after the eighth ring and circled **Cartcher, WD** and made a note to call the number again later. She dropped her feet back on the floor, scooted the chair closer to the desk, and re-read the stories on the discovery of the body of the Jane Doe, later identified as Millicent Cartcher of Clarion, Georgia, though it was stretching a point to call them "stories." They were brief paragraphs of several sentences each that had been buried deep within the metro section of the paper, the first one running on a Sunday. She looked again at the date. Almost a year ago:

The body of an unidentified
female was discovered behind
the Southwest Waterfront Marina
early yesterday morning. The
white female, approximately
fifty years old, was fully clothed
and appeared to have been
strangled. Police say there
were no signs of a struggle or
of sexual abuse. There was
no identification with the body
or identifying marks on the
body.

And a month later, this:

Police still have not identified
the body of a female found
behind the Southwest Water-
front Marina last month. A
forensic examination places
the woman's age between 45
and 55 years old. She had
been dead less than 24 hours
when she was discovered.
Police have released an artist's
rendering of the victim and ask
that anyone with knowledge
of the woman's identity call...

And almost seven months later:

*Police have identified the
body of a woman found five
months ago at the Southwest
Waterfront as 54-year old
Millicent Cartcher of Reston,
VA, who had recently moved to
the area from Georgia. She was
strangled to death. Police have
no motive for the slaying, and
no suspects.*

"And what else is new," Mimi muttered, not at all embarrassed that she'd been overheard by at least four other reporters. If talking to oneself was the strangest thing a reporter ever did, they'd have to be considered almost normal. She'd called all the Cartchers listed in four different Georgia area codes, assuming that such an unusual surname wouldn't be common and, therefore, that bearers of the same name would be related to the late Millicent. None of the dead woman's relatives was pleased to hear from a Washington reporter asking questions more than a year after the fact. Not even non-relatives, including the editor of the weekly newspaper in Clarion, were willing to spend longer on the telephone than the several seconds it took for Mimi to identify herself and the reason for her call. She needed an atlas; she needed to find out exactly where Clarion was. She had relatives in Atlanta and she didn't think it was near there. And she needed to pay a visit to Reston. Perhaps a neighbor would remember--

"Patterson." She snatched up her phone in the middle of the first ring, and instantly regretted it. Gianna was on the other end, tearing into her about interfering and meddling and being a general nuisance. Not that she considered posing a few questions "meddling," though she'd like to have known how Gianna found out so quickly. Then she remembered her conversation with Renee. She'd have told Marianne and Marianne would have told

57

Gianna. Before Mimi could think of something to say to unruffle her feathers, Gianna cancelled their dinner plans for the evening, said she didn't know when she'd be home and hung up, leaving Mimi listening to a dial tone.

"Story of my life," Mimi muttered, dropping the phone into its cradle.

"What are you grousing about now, Patterson?"

"Leave me alone, Tyler."

He stood in front of her desk looking down at her and there was something in his gaze that erased the unease and irritation that she felt. She looked at Tyler and found comfort in who and what he was, in the steady green eyes behind the tortoise shell glasses, the khaki slacks and white shirt and brown tie that he wore every day. He was predictable, yes: predictably honest and fair and above reproach. "So, tell me, Tyler, when did I lose my humanity? Or at least the ability to write from a human perspective?"

He raised his eyebrows at her. "Who's been talking to you?"

"Nobody talks to me any more, Tyler, you should know that. And the only expectation anybody has of me is that I'll keep sending corrupt government officials to jail. But nobody really cares about that any more. Which is sending me messages I'd really rather not hear."

"Jesus, Patterson," he said sadly. "You really do need to get away."

"Yeah, I know. But Gianna can't go and I can't think of anyplace I'd want to go alone. And anyway, the Weasel hasn't signed off on my vacation request."

"Follow me," he ordered, and scurried off between the desks and toward the hallway leading to the cafeteria. She sat for a moment, then stood and followed. He was waiting for her by the water cooler, their spot for clandestine conversations, literally tapping his foot at her languid approach.

"If you're going to try to make me feel better, Tyler,

58

thanks but no thanks."

"Don't talk, Patterson, just listen. First, the Weasel okayed your VR this morning, effective Friday." And then Tyler suggested that she hang out with friends of his who'd just bought a villa— that's what he called it— on Florida's Gulf coast. She remembered his friends, Sue and Kate. She'd met them once, at a party at Tyler's. At the time, they lived in Baltimore and worked in D.C. Tyler said they made a killing in the tech market, saw the crash coming and got out ahead of the disaster with real money, and lots of it. Quit their government jobs and retired a full ten years ahead of their contemporaries.

"You think they'd have me? I mean, I really don't know them. I only met them that one time."

"You complicate everything unnecessarily, Mimi. Why is that?"

She pondered the question and a possible answer and came up blank. "I don't know. Habit, I guess. So, OK, Sue and Kate."

"I'll call them tonight and set it up."

"Thanks, Tyler,"

He touched her arm and walked away.

CHAPTER FIVE

Mimi and Gianna both were uncomfortable with the way things were left between them, but there wasn't time to work through their difficulties in the days prior to Mimi's departure for Florida. Though they both claimed that the week's separation would do them good, neither of them believed it. How could it? If they couldn't find the time to talk while in the same city, often under the same roof, how would being separated by hundreds of miles help? It was an asinine situation, and thinking about it on the flight down to Florida didn't do Mimi much good. But talking about it did, she was surprised to discover. Almost as surprised as when she found herself talking freely and openly to Sue and Kate about the complex nature of her relationship with Gianna.

They'd met Gianna the same time they met Mimi and remembered her, in Sue's words, as "pretty, polite, intense, and distant. I didn't know she was a cop until later, but when I found out, it fit. She was very...um... watchful."

Mimi was comfortable with Sue and Kate and relaxed and comfortable in their home. And why not? Tyler's description of the place as a villa wasn't far off the mark. They lived in Dunedin, Florida, on the Gulf of Mexico, in a house that was as much external as internal, in that it was constructed around a pool and courtyard, with palm trees as sentries and bougainvillea and birds of paradise as attendants. Mimi had her own room and bath and private patio with pool access, so she could be alone as much as she liked. But she found that she enjoyed spending time with her hostesses.

Sue, a tall, gangly woman with frizzy salt-and-cayenne pepper-colored hair, was an accountant with an office at home. She played golf every morning at first light, and drank coffee and read three newspapers on the terrace overlooking the Gulf afterwards. Kate, shorter and rounder and the kind of pretty that prompted double-takes, worked three days a week in an antique store and volunteered two days a week in an AIDS hospice in Tampa, and was home only in the evenings. So, by default, Mimi spent most mornings with Sue and most evenings with Kate.

Mimi usually bristled when she heard other people's comments about Gianna, usually because they rarely were complimentary, but she hadn't minded Sue's observation. It was, after all, accurate. And she hadn't objected at dinner her second evening with them when Kate had probed her about the workings of their relationship. That's when she had spilled all— the beans and her guts. Sue and Kate received her outpouring with warmth and without judgment and offered a single piece of advice: relationships are what you make them.

"I'd think that would be obvious," Mimi had responded, working to cover her amusement at so transparent a statement pronounced with such gravity.

"You'd think," Kate had replied dryly, not seeming at all amused.

"I think a lot of people believe that once they're in a relationship, it'll behave the way they imagine relationships do or should, without understanding that each couple is responsible for creating the relationship that works best for the two of them," Sue offered thoughtfully, and poured the rest of the wine into her glass.

"Jesus, Sue!" Kate exclaimed through an exhalation of cigarette smoke. "You sound like a self-help tape."

Sue gave her a good-natured smile. "Maybe so, but I'm right, aren't I?"

Kate nodded. "I suppose. Just see if you can't find some different words to say it next time, OK?"

Now Sue snorted. "What next time? Mimi's the only person who's been either polite enough or interested enough or non-threatened enough for this kind of conversation in ages." And as if on cue, both looked questioningly at her, though it took her a moment to realize it because she was buttering an ear of corn— her third.

"You want to know if I'm polite?" Mimi asked, chewing and talking at the same time. "I guess I'm more interested and non-threatened," she added, still talking with her mouth full. "Though I'm thinking now that maybe I don't really know what you meant, exactly."

Sue further explained herself: "All couples have areas of disagreement, and the only way to prevent those areas from becoming battlefields is to work through them, or to agree that they're always going to be disagreements and agree to accept them— and to stay the hell away from them. You and Gianna haven't done that yet."

"No shit," Mimi agreed, managing to smile through the discomfort the revelation brought. "We're definitely still at the battlefield stage in some areas of our relationship." Like discussing our work with each other, she thought.

Kate had stood and begun clearing the table.
"Don't press her any more, Sue, this isn't an easy conversation to have, as you well know."

Sue had stiffened slightly and was momentarily silent before opening another bottle of wine and resuming conversation on a different topic. But Mimi had noticed and wondered, and then dismissed the episode, concentrating instead on the sun setting over the Gulf and on the wine and on trying to remember when she'd eaten three ears of corn at one sitting. Later, her focus was on getting through the pile of books borrowed from Sue and Kate's well-stocked library. She was taking Tyler at his word and relishing every moment of it. She went to the golf course with Sue and thoroughly enjoyed the world at daybreak, as she did the early morning golfers: three other women, one of whom clearly was more than just a friend to Sue. The following day she spent with Kate, discovering that the antique store where she worked she also owned, and that she made the drive to Tampa in order to get stuck in traffic, as much as to be of service to the dying. "I don't miss the grind of a day job," she told Mimi, "but I do miss big city energy. I know it sounds really crazy to say, but the traffic jams help relieve the little twinges of homesickness I feel for the East Coast." Then she peered through the windshield at the bumper- to-bumper traffic surrounding them and gave a bark of laughter. "And this ain't even real traffic, considering that mess on 495."

Mimi agreed. The parking lot that was the Washington Beltway was notoriously and habitually jammed, and Mimi always swore she'd either change jobs or change residences if ever she found herself required to traverse its eight lanes twice a day. "I refuse to get on the thing, but I went to school in Los Angeles and I remember traffic jams." She pushed the button that lowered her window as Kate lit a cigarette, and Mimi realized that it was only since she'd begun frequenting a bar again that she ever encountered people who smoked. Kate noticed and stubbed the cigarette out in the ashtray.

"Sorry. I'm not used to having somebody else in the car."

"Sue doesn't mind?" she asked, and Kate shrugged, prompting Mimi to probe before she realized what she was doing. "Does that mean you care that the smoke bothers me, but you don't care if it bothers Sue?"

"It means that Sue drinks and I smoke," Kate said with another shrug, and Mimi left it alone, though she wondered, just as she had wondered the night before when Kate had terminated the discussion at the dinner table. There definitely was a battlefield- caliber issue lurking beneath the surface of the Sue-Kate relationship, but that was none of Mimi's business. She had her own problems. Besides, she was enjoying herself on this stolen vacation. She liked both Sue and Kate, and hoped that this visit would develop into a friendship, because she thought that Gianna would like them, too. She knew that they missed the D.C.-Baltimore area and she was prepared to welcome them as guests in her home on their visits east. The last thing she wanted was to be placed in the middle of a domestic dispute, especially one in which it was necessary to take sides.

"I'd like to take you and Sue to dinner tonight."

"Thanks, Mimi, but we'd kind of planned a little surprise for your last night with us," Kate said, her voice definitely holding a hint of a surprise.

"Oh. Well." Mimi certainly was surprised, and that was without knowing what it was. "In that case, I'm entirely at your disposal."

"Good," Kate said with enthusiasm. "I'm going to drop you off at home and I've got two quick stops to make, then I'll be along." She was turning into the street that led to the waterway that led to their enclave. It was, Mimi thought again, a beautiful place and way to live, though she also wondered, again, whether it would or could ever be the life for her. When she looked at Sue and Kate, she didn't see old...she didn't see "retired." They both were fifty-five and alive, vibrant, active, fully engaged in life and living. They were wealthy women enjoying the benefits of their wealth. But there was a "but" in the equation for Mimi, and she couldn't pinpoint it; couldn't shake off the feeling that she should care. Why should she? It wasn't her life and it didn't have to be. No law required that at a given age, she must "retire" and live differently from the way she lived now. As sick as she was of ferreting out graft and corruption and sending scumbags to jail, she didn't want to leave Washington and her life there.

Those thoughts held her as she traversed the walkway, opened the front door, and entered the house, and it took her a moment to understand what she was looking at through the expanse of interior glass that opened onto the pool and the courtyard. "Oh, shit," she muttered when she realized that she'd stumbled upon Sue in a hot embrace with her golf partner. "Damn!" There was no way to get to her room without being seen, though Sue and what's-her-name definitely weren't interested in her. She took a couple of backward steps, thinking she could leave, but the motion must have caught Sue's eye

64

because she stepped out of the lip-lock she was in and looked directly toward Mimi. Then she smiled and gestured that Mimi should come out. "What the hell is the matter with her?" Mimi muttered, taking tiny, reluctant steps toward the sliding glass doors leading to the courtyard. Why would someone caught in the clutches of an illicit affair be smiling about it? Mimi opened the door and stepped from the interior coolness into the warm outside air.

"Mimi," Sue said without a hint of embarrassment in her voice. "I didn't expect you back so early. Where's Kate?"

"She had a couple of errands to run so she dropped me off. She'll be back shortly."

Sue waved off the explanation. "You remember Lynne?"

Mimi nodded. She remembered Lynne though she hadn't remembered her name. Dark-haired, dark-eyed, tanned bronze, tall and athletic. She and Lynne nodded a greeting at each other, and Lynne turned away and sauntered toward the door to Sue's office. Had they anticipated Mimi's arrival, Lynne could have disappeared without a trace; Sue's office had a private entrance from the side of the house. "Sorry," Mimi said when Lynne was gone.

"Sorry for what?" Surprise and dismay spread across Sue's face, and instantly were replaced by the embarrassment that had been absent a moment ago. "I'm the one who's sorry, Mimi. I didn't realize you didn't know."

"How would I know?" Mimi asked curtly, annoyed now by Sue's casual attitude. Why the hell would she know about Sue's affair with Lynne?

"Since you spent the day with Kate, I thought she would have told you about Lynne," Sue replied in answer to the question Mimi had thought but not voiced. "But it seems she let you discover for yourself and left the explaining to me."

Now Mimi was pissed as well as confused. "I really don't want to be in the middle of whatever is going on here, Sue."

"You're not in the middle of anything, Mimi. We should

have done a better job of explaining."

Mimi shook her head and wished she could evaporate. "You don't owe me any explanation for how you live your lives. I appreciate your hospitality. I've truly enjoyed being here--"

"--and the reason we wanted to explain," Sue said, interrupting, pleading in her expression and her voice, "is because we like and enjoy you, and we want you as a friend. You and Gianna. So, can we sit and talk and I can explain this?" She gestured toward the pool and the chaise lounges. Mimi, who'd worn a bathing suit constantly since her arrival, had planned on a swim anyway.

"Sure," she said, pulling her tee shirt over her head and stepping out of her shorts and reluctantly dropping down on to a chaise, but ready to dive into head first into the pool to escape whatever was coming if necessary.

Sue sat down opposite her. "In a nutshell, Kate and I don't have sex together any more. Kate's choice, not mine; I feel sexier now than I did twenty years ago. So, I can leave Kate, or stay and find sex elsewhere. Ergo, Lynne."

"Whew!" was Mimi's reaction.

"Yeah, that's kinda how I feel about it," Sue said.

"You're not happy with this arrangement." It was not a question but Sue shook her head in reply as if it were, then she shrugged, but didn't speak. "So, why," Mimi began, then found she didn't know where to go from there. She felt very much out of her element in this discussion.

"What else can I do, Mimi? What would you do? I don't want to leave Sue. Not only do I love her, I like her better than anybody I've ever known. She's my best friend, closest confidant, and a true partner."

Mimi hesitated, and then asked, "What happened? Kate wasn't always uninterested in sex, was she?"

Sadness closed Sue's face. "This has been going on for the last two years or so, thanks to menopause." Then she laughed and the sadness vanished. "Don't look so terrified, Mimi, loss of libido isn't every woman's fate, though there aren't any absolutes in menopause, and no rules. It happens differently for every woman, and fortunately there are herbs and other stuff to ease most of the symptoms."

"Then why doesn't Kate take something?"

"That's the problem, dammit! Kate hates everything about menopause. She's taking it personally— the weight gain, the loss of libido, the mood swings— the nerve of Nature doing these things to her! Tell you the truth, Mimi, Kate still hasn't recovered from being fifty. She's not aging gracefully. Almost every conversation has some reference to when she was thirty or forty, and she won't even acknowledge a birthday."

"And so you just don't talk about the problem any more?" Mimi asked. "You're just letting all this stuff hang there while you're doing Lynne and Kate's doing nothing?"

Sue sighed and suddenly looked very tired. "I think one of her close friends finally has convinced her to see a therapist. She's older and wiser and Kate trusts her. But if that fails, there's not much else I can do."

"Sure there is," Mimi retorted. "You can find another lover."

"That's the first dumb thing you've said," Sue shot back, taking Mimi totally by surprise. "I'm fifty-five years old. Where am I going to find another partner, somebody I can like *and* love? When was the last time you saw an unattached fifty- something lesbian?"

Sue and Kate's surprise for Mimi was a good-bye dinner-pool party. They'd invited a couple dozen men and women, set up three gas grills at different intervals in the courtyard, turned on the speakers, and got a full-fledged party going. Mimi was glad she'd had the chance to practice some dance steps at *The Bayou*, though even with her practice she found it difficult to keep pace with a couple of her partners. When dancing required more energy than she had left, Mimi fell into the pool, along with half a dozen others, and floated on the water's surface, gazing at the sky and wishing Gianna were here with her. Then she climbed out of the water and ate until she was too full to move, which left her at the mercy of a table of storytellers whose expertise was tall tales, if one were generous, lies if one were truthful. She laughed until her sides hurt. It was an eclectic group of people— the eldest probably in her seventies, the youngest probably hadn't had his twenty-fifth birthday— and they all seemed to know and enjoy each other. Mimi was beginning to understand the dilemma facing her new friends: it would not be an easy thing to walk away from this life, from this circle of friends.

By midnight, just Sue, Kate, Mimi, and two other women— Sarah and Cissy— were left, both of whom were former D.C. residents who had visited Florida for the first time the previous year and, as a result, had quit their jobs, sold their house, and moved south. Mimi wondered briefly if they still were lovers, then banished the thought. They knew of Mimi's work, they said, and Gianna's, too, but rather than comment on some aspect of newspaper or police work, as Mimi expected and was braced for, they asked for her help: find out what happened to their missing friend.

"She can't do that!" Kate exclaimed.

"Why not?" Sue asked, pouncing on the notion like a hungry predator. "It never crossed my mind to ask, but it's a damn good idea and I wish I'd thought of it. Could you look into it, Mimi? We'd sure appreciate it."

"Look into what, exactly?" Mimi asked cautiously.

"Sarah's friend, Ellie Litton, disappeared without a trace. One minute she's bought a new house, a new car, new clothes, hell, a whole new life, and the next minute she's gone. Vanished into thin air, like a character in a 1920's British murder mystery." Sue clearly was upset, as were Kate and their friends, especially Sarah who had known Ellie since they were girls in Iowa and had kept in touch over the years, thrilled to discover, as adults, that both were lesbians.

Mimi's antennae were fully at attention. "Disappeared from where? And what did you say her name was?"

Eric Ashby slapped the conference table with the palm of his hand, making a sharp, loud noise that irritated Gianna, though she understood both why he was upset and why she allowed herself to be annoyed by his display of pique. Marianne had indeed recognized Ellie's photo but knew nothing more about her. "Ellie Litton's her name and it's a damn good thing she had the kind of job that required a security clearance, because we probably never would have found out who she was otherwise!" There now were six murdered women presumed to be lesbians and they'd identified only two of them: Millicent Cartcher and Ellie Litton. The company that Ellie worked for had contracts with the military, requiring that its top computer people undergo security checks, which included fingerprints on file; otherwise, Ellie likely would have remained a Jane Doe forever. Or at least as long as Millicent Cartcher had.

Cassie, Kenny and Linda had combed the files Gianna had brought from the Medical Examiner's office and concluded that not only was there potentially a very big problem confronting them, it also was too big for the three of them work alone. "If it's true that all these women are lesbians, Boss..." Cassie shivered. "I don't even want to think about what that means."

"I don't, either," Kenny and Linda said in unison, and Gianna took their meaning. Neither of them were lesbians and they were unnerved by what they were finding in the files.

Gianna had to decide quickly, not only what to do, but how to do it. She was walking bare-assed in a minefield and if she stumbled there would be no salvation. Not following through on the Irish guns was not an option; the chief would fire her for that. But conscience would not let her ignore the possibility that someone was targeting lesbians for murder. She might be able to manage her resources well enough to work both cases, but how would she manage the jurisdictional problem without involving

69

the chief? He'd fire her for that, too, if she got caught. And she had a jurisdictional problem of gargantuan proportions. Millicent Cartcher had lived in Virginia and Ellie Litton had lived in Maryland and both were murdered in D.C., but on Federal property, which made them matters for the Feds. But Gianna wanted these cases. She believed she could successfully argue that the murders were hate crimes if she could prove that all the women were lesbians, and that their sexual identity was the reason for their murders. But she couldn't do that without knowing the identity of the other victims, and there didn't seem to be much hope for that after so much time had elapsed. But first things first.

She pulled Eric from the guns investigation to supervise Cassie, Kenny and Linda. Alice Long would be a swing member of that team because she was a lesbian and could traverse the terrain, though nobody else knew that, and Gianna didn't intend to reveal the fact. It would cause discomfort for Cassie, and Gianna didn't want that. But because Alice also had a handle on the operation of the Jamaican drug dealers who were after the Irish guns, she'd have to keep one eye on that investigation, and be back-up for Bobby. Which left Tim without back-up. And which left Gianna, herself, to play that role. And to some how keep them all from getting blown to smithereens if she made a misstep and landed on a live mine.

"We've got to get into Ellie Litton's place."

Eric nodded. "I know, Boss, I'm working on it."

"And we've got to talk to the personnel people where she worked."

"I've got an appointment first thing Monday morning."

"And who are these other women? How can so many women be dead and nobody cares? I've got to believe that at least one of them lived in the city, and I want to know the who and the where--"

"But those cases are all older and colder than Cartcher. So what good does that do us?" Cassie asked, too intense to worry

70

about interrupting her boss. "Even if we find 'em, Boss, there won't be any evidence left for us to investigate. Their places would have been cleaned out months ago."

"But it'll give us a legitimate reason to nose around in the other cases, those that don't belong to us," Gianna replied.

"I wish we didn't have to keep going through this," Kenny groused. "Nobody wants these cases, nobody gives a shit about the vics but us, but we keep having to prove ourselves, to earn the right to claim the investigations..." Kenny let the argument go. It was an old, familiar one and nobody needed to hear it again, especially since everyone in the room agreed with him.

They were seated around the conference table in the Think Tank, a stack of files in front of each of them as voluminous as those piled atop each of the five desks. It was Friday evening, way past quitting time; way past dinner time. They all were exhausted and ravenous, yet they couldn't leave. Didn't want to leave. At least, not to go home; and they all were too tired to do more work. Bobby and Alice had staked out the Eight Rivers bar until after two that morning, the same time Tim had left the Shamrock, and they reported that drunk Irishmen and drunk Jamaicans stumbled home to their respective abodes, the only guns visible those in their pockets. No sign of a cache of illegal weapons. Cassie and Linda had bar-hopped, too, until well after midnight, without finding anyone who recognized Ellie Litton's photograph, or anyone who was aware of anyone who'd disappeared. Gianna, Eric and Kenny had spent most of the night sifting through the files in the medical examiner's office for the third night in a row, and marveled that cases ever went to trial in the city with sufficient forensic evidence.

Gianna had had several conversations with the ME, and had secured his grudging support for treating the six cases as hate crimes, and the six women as victims of the same killer. While he wasn't willing to stipulate that all six were lesbians, he agreed that the fact that all six had been garroted, that two of them had intact hymen and another two were without evidence of recent vaginal penetration, was more than mere coincidence. "But what I really want to know," he growled at her, "is why the hell the murdering son of a bitch left 'em here for us to deal with!"

Gianna thought she knew the answer to that one, but since she needed his cooperation, she refrained from sharing what she was thinking. After all, it wasn't his fault that the meddling bureaucrats in the Federal Government never budgeted sufficient funds for the city to properly function. And anyway, she was glad "the murdering son of a bitch," whoever he— or she— was, left the victims for D.C. to deal with since D.C. was the only local jurisdiction with a separate Hate Crimes Unit. Not that anybody willingly gave them their due...but they'd already proven their worth. They'd apprehended the woman who, driven by revenge and insanity, had mutilated and murdered five wealthy, deep-in-the-closet homosexuals, and the bored rich boys who made the killing of prostitutes an initiation rite into their group. All of those murders were committed in D.C., giving the Hate Crimes Unit jurisdiction, even though none of the murderers lived in the city. In this case— and Gianna was calling it a case— the murders all occurred in D.C., though deliberately on Federal property, which Gianna thought...believed...felt...meant the perpetrator knew enough local law to know that the half dozen or so local enforcement agencies got in each other's way more than they helped each other.

Alice said, "You think the perp knows a lot about the city and about the law don't you, Lieutenant?"

Gianna gave her a long, hard look, and Alice held it. She wasn't much older than Bobby or Kenny or Linda, but she was much more experienced, having spent most of her career in a variety of undercover assignments. Alice Long was a good cop, smart and tough and resourceful and, apparently, insightful. "The thought crossed my mind."

"And smart enough to target women who live in the 'burbs, lure 'em into the city, and kill 'em on Federal property,

72

screwing up the jurisdictional authority?" she asked in a musing tone.

"No asshole perp's that smart!" Bobby shot at Alice, and they all looked to Gianna for confirmation of his assertion.

"Depends on the perp," she said slowly, "and what he's after." She wasn't ready to have this conversation. She'd been mulling over a few possibilities, but nothing had taken shape or form yet. She changed the subject. "Cassie, tell me again exactly what you've got on the possible girlfriend of the Cartcher woman."

Cassie dug her notebook out of her purse, flipped some pages, read for a moment, then repeated what she'd heard from Marianne and three other witnesses. Before they opened *The Bayou,* Marianne and Renee had owned a bar in Columbia, Maryland, *Happy Landings,* which drew its patrons primarily from Baltimore and surrounding Maryland towns, and most of whom were older, professional women. Marianne met Millie Cartcher in March or April of last year— nineteen months ago. She came into the bar three or four nights a week, and was warm and outgoing, a real Southern charmer. She liked people and people liked her but she'd never go out with anyone, giving Marianne the impression that she was involved with someone. Her intuition was proved correct, Marianne said, on the first mild day of the season, when the patio was opened. On that evening, Marianne brought Millie's whiskey sour out to the patio. She said Millie was flushed and excited, but the bar was busy and Marianne didn't have time to chat. Then, about an hour later, remembering that she hadn't seen her, Marianne returned to the patio, to find Millicent in a lip-lock with a woman she hadn't seen before.

Gianna interrupted. "When does it get warm enough for restaurants to open their patios and gardens?"

"After last winter? The first day it was warmer than freezing!" Eric said, and made a note to himself to check with the weather service for last year's first sign of spring in Columbia.

"So," Gianna mused, "Millie Cartcher began frequenting

Happy Landings in Columbia, Maryland, when she's just bought a beautiful condo on the lake in Reston, Virginia— how many miles away? And on the other side of the Potomac, a hellish drive either out 495 or across the Woodrow Wilson Bridge. Who in their right mind would do that three or four times a week? Aren't there any women's bars in Virginia?"

"Nope," Eric, Cassie, Kenny and Linda said in unison, surprising Gianna and interrupting her thought flow momentarily. "You've gotta go to Richmond to find a women's bar in Virginia," Cassie added.

"Which would probably be a much shorter drive from Reston than driving all the way to Columbia," Alice threw in, again following Gianna's thought pattern.

"So, Millie drives to Columbia from Reston to have a drink, and meets a woman who's also a stranger to the bar. And then, a few months later, Ellie Litton leaves Iowa and moves..."

"To Columbia!" Cassie shouted. "Just about the time Millie Cartcher's body was found behind the marina!"

Silence reigned and Gianna was grateful for it. She'd done too much talking before she was ready. She'd been trying to fit all the pieces together in her mind, and what was taking shape definitely was ugly, though it still largely was unformed.

She was developing a physical description of the six women whose files they had pulled, and cataloging all the information from the post mortems and the death certificates. The similarities were striking. The six victims all were in their fifties— the youngest, according to the ME, about fifty-three and the eldest close to sixty. Four of them were white and two were Black and all had been killed from behind, without a struggle, by a length of piano wire stretched so tightly around their necks as to sever the esophagus; and the two who were identified were new arrivals to the area, leading directly to the speculation that the others were strangers, too, since their bodies hadn't been identified or claimed. And both known victims had ties to Marianne's bars.

"Forget about the bar hopping," Gianna said to Cassie and

Linda, "and focus on *The Bayou.*" Then another thought stopped her. "Marianne and Renee sold that place in Columbia, they didn't close it." She looked at Bobby. "You're going to have to go solo on the Jamaicans for the time being, but do it from a distance. Do not, under any circumstances, go inside that bar alone. I'll get you some backup." Then she looked at Alice, who was looking at her, nodding.

"I'm already there, Lieutenant. I want to find out for myself how long it takes to drive from Reston to Columbia. I'm sure the bartender fixes a mean drink, but I'm betting that only a lover would make somebody drive that distance that often."

Bobby, who so far had contributed little to the discussion, raised the index finger on his right hand— after first giving the knuckles a good crack— his signal that his thoughts were formulated and he was ready to speak. "And maybe that lover was tired of making that trip all the way to Columbia, too. Boss, I'm thinking like Long Legs on this one, that our killer has ties to the city, and I'd sure as hell rather be looking for his ass than sitting on some damn Jamaican drug dealers!"

"If it's a lover, it ain't a he, Gilliam," Cassie said, and Bobby gave her a look. "You said you'd rather be looking for 'his' ass. We're talking about lesbians. Their lovers would be shes, not hes."

Bobby snorted. "What kind of woman would be strong enough to sever somebody's esophagus with a length of piano wire?" He caught looks from Cassie, Alice and Gianna that stopped him for a moment, but only for a moment. "I don't buy it. I don't buy that a woman is doing these killings."

"Women get more like men every day, Bobby, and that's no compliment," Linda said, launching a discussion that supported itself without Gianna's intervention or participation. Gianna welcomed the respite. She was really feeling the negative effects of having too many thoughts and not enough time and space in which to process them. And now there was the focus on Marianne and *The Bayou.* Not that Marianne was a suspect, but

75

her bar was, and she needed to talk to her about that. But not at the bar, and before Mimi returned.

The thought of Mimi caused her breath to catch in her chest. They hadn't talked for three days, largely because Gianna had been working practically around the clock and had not been in a private enough environment for a real conversation, even on her cell phone. Mimi was angry with her for not making the time to talk, and she was, if not angry with Mimi, at least still annoyed that she had questioned Renee about Millicent Cartcher. But mostly she missed her, and would be glad to see her and be with her.

Everybody in the room jumped when the phone rang, then they all checked their watches. It was after nine on a Friday night. They looked quizzically at each other, then at the phone. Just before the third ring, Eric answered it, and they all watched his face change expressions, their own registering a variety of emotions, ranging from apprehension (Tim, Linda and Alice), to excitement (Cassie, Bobby and Kenny), to dread (Gianna.) He said, "Yes, Sir," three times, and after the final time, added, "She's right here. I'll tell her right now and she'll be on her way."

"I'm on my way where?" Gianna asked as Eric hung up the phone.

"To the ME's. That was Shehee. He's got another one, and this one's ours. She was found in an alley a block from *The Bayou* early this morning by a sanitation crew."

76

CHAPTER SIX

The chief was raising hell and there was nothing Gianna could do but sit and take it. He was telling her, for the third time, how she should kneel down and thank the Almighty that she hadn't caused any jurisdictional problems for him— and for herself— by launching an unauthorized investigation into the murders of Millicent Cartcher and Ellie Litton, no matter that the Cartcher case was inactive in Fairfax County, Virginia or that the Litton case had barely rippled the waters in Frederick County, Maryland, or that the Park Police didn't even know what he was talking about when he broached the subject with them. He had talked to the chiefs in all three jurisdictions and formally indicated an interest in the cases and requested their cooperation, based on the discovery Thursday morning of the Jane Doe in D.C., and on the Medical Examiner's conclusion that the latest victim was part of a pattern— a previously determined pattern— of potential victims of hate crimes. He had done everything but lie to conceal the fact of her previous involvement in their jurisdictions, and she was lucky that his good rapport with the other chiefs meant that they took him at his word. He didn't tell her, because he didn't need to, that the other three chiefs welcomed his intervention because they had more than enough to worry about on their own without some dead lesbian Jane Does to gum up the works. But their indifference to the murders of the six women only served to fuel the fire he had burning.

"And if you ever make this kind of mess for me again, Maglione, I personally will walk your papers over to the retirement board and watch while somebody accepts 'em, if I have to sign 'em myself."

"Yes, sir," she said, waiting to see if he was finished or if there was rant and rave still left within him. It was hard to tell because he was pacing back and forth, hands stuffed into his pockets jiggling the change. Damn, she hated it when he did that.

"Any word on the ID of the woman?"

She nodded. She, Cassie, Linda and Alice had descended on *The Bayou* within moments after receiving the call from the ME and, armed with a verbal description of the victim, had canvassed the place, which was packed to the rafters on a Friday night. Marianne, Renee, Trudi the bartenders, and Peggy, the *doyenne* of the piano bar, all identified the victim, based on the verbal description, as Sandy Somebody, newly arrived in D.C. from one of the upstate New York college towns— Buffalo, Albany, Syracuse— and that she lived in the general vicinity of the bar. She was "fifty-something" and a college professor, Trudi the bartender thought at Morgan State University in Baltimore, though Peggy the singer believed at Howard University in D.C. It was certain, though, that Sandy had been in *The Bayou* on the previous night; Peggy said she'd been in the lounge listening to her sing and play. All agreed that Sandy was pretty and pleasant but shy and a bit reserved.

"Goddammit! Some son of a bitch is luring these women here to kill them! What the hell kind of sense does that make? If the bastard just wants to kill somebody, why not kill people already here? What do you make of this one, Maglione?" And he looked at her as if he really expected a rational response.

I don't make anything of it, Chief. Not yet."

"Well, you'd better, and soon. He's killed two women in less than a month, when it was taking him at least six months before, which means he's starting to unravel, and you know what that means."

"You keep saying 'he,' Chief."

"Damn right. This isn't a woman's crime, Maglione, yoking people from behind, not to mention being strong enough to cut a wind pipe in half. A man's doing these murders."

Gianna squeezed her eyes shut and massaged her temples. She wished she could agree with him. "These victims were all

78

lesbians, or at least frequented a lesbian bar on a regular basis. Three of them were seen in intimate circumstances with women, and no men have been inside either of the bars in question. Everything points to a woman perp."

He shook his head in disgust. "These are men's crimes, and you know it."

"What I know is that women get more like men every day," she replied, quoting Linda Lopez and receiving the same deadening silence that Linda had drawn. "I agree that it would require a woman of considerable physical strength, but there are women more than capable, Chief, and you know that."

"What I know is that I want those damn guns, and Goddammit, I want whoever is bringing women to my town just to kill 'em! I'll give you every resource on this one, Maglione."

"I'm glad to hear you say that, Sir, because resources definitely will be required. We're going to have to backtrack these women to their local addresses and to their hometowns."

"You can have Tony Watkins back. Put him with Gilliam on the Jamaicans. He knows as much about them as Long does, since they worked that undercover drug task force together. Long'll be more useful to you on the lesbian angle anyway."

She gave him a hard look. Did he know Alice was a lesbian? And if so, how? Probably the same way he knew about her, though she never was certain that he did. How would he know? And why would he care? He had too many other things to think about than which of his cops were gay, though his facility for knowing everything about everything was legendary. And as if to demonstrate the point, he asked, "Where's your girlfriend, and are we going to be able to keep her out of our cases and keep our cases out of her newspaper for a change?"

The truth was that Gianna didn't know where her girlfriend was. She'd received a message from Mimi that she had missed her Sunday afternoon flight and that she'd catch the next available plane. It now was Monday morning. She'd worked all night and endured a dressing down by the chief, and she still hadn't heard from Mimi. She'd left messages at both her own home and at Mimi's, and on Mimi's cell phone and office phone voice mails, saying that she was working all night, and she'd called several times to see if Mimi had arrived. Now, in addition to being sleepy, hungry and irritable, she was worried about Mimi. Where the hell was she? She had turned in her rental car— this Gianna knew because she could check rental car records. What she could not do— would not do— was call Sue and Kate or Tyler and ask where Mimi was. She'd wait until nine o'clock and call her at work, where she would be if everything was all right.

She had showered and changed clothes and had managed to down a cup of coffee before her meeting with the chief. She'd dearly have loved a workout, but she'd settle for more coffee and something to eat. The coffee was easy. She poured herself another cup from the pot she'd made before her meeting with the chief. Food was another matter. She shared Mimi's feelings about eating anything from the department cafeteria, including what dropped from the metal hooks in the vending machines on the first floor, but there wasn't enough time to go out for anything and be back in time for her morning meeting with the Unit. Dammit, if she hadn't had to listen to the chief rant and rave for the better part of an hour....

"Come in!" she called out in response to the rapid-fire rapping at her door, and Eric charged in, bleary-eyed from lack of sleep but bristling with the energy of newly-discovered information to impart. She noticed, not for the first time, that the stubble on his unshaven face produced hair much darker that the bright red hair on his head; but she also noticed— for the very first time— a few white hairs sprinkled among the dark, reddish brown ones. She waved him toward the couch and as he sank down, she poured him a cup of coffee, remembering how young they were when they'd met and become instant friends at the police academy. Aware, owing to the white in his beard and to the silver strands in her own auburn hair, of how many years ago that was.

"Sandra Phillips," he said stifling a yawn and accepting the mug of coffee from her. "We found her car a block from the bar. Big, shiny, brand new Cadillac."

"Do we know where she lives?" Sandra Phillips had been dead for a little more than seventy-two hours. Getting inside her residence, gaining access to the details of her personal, intimate life, was crucial, and every lapsed minute literally could mean the difference between apprehending her murderer and not. Gianna knew Eric knew this, knew that he was talking about the car because that was all he had to talk about at the moment. But she had to ask, just as she had to feel the disappointment at the answer she knew was coming.

He was shaking his head. "It's still got New York tags, but we're getting close. The canvass turned up three people who'd seen the car recently— all of 'em ex-New Yorkers who notice things like New York tags— and the parking enforcement agent who wrote three tickets on it since Thursday night for being parked in a Residential Permit Zone. He thinks the car lives near East Capitol and Eighth." He drained his cup and stood up.

"By the way, I heard from my friend in Maryland, the one who took a look inside Ellie Litton's house for me? Empty as a church on Monday. The way he pieced it together, a week after her body was found, a moving van showed up and emptied out the place, didn't even leave a dust ball. So, yeah, we've gotta find Sandy's place ASAP."

"And I know you will, Eric. But first, my friend, you'll go home and get yourself cleaned up, maybe get a nap."

"I'm all right, Anna.."

"But you look like crap. Go on, I'll hold down the fort until you get back." She walked to the door with him.

He opened the door to leave, then turned to look back at her, making no effort to smother the yawn that stretched his face. "And you look marvelous, as always."

"Thanks pal," Gianna said, stifling her own yawn.

She poured herself another cup of coffee and dropped into the chair behind the desk, back aching with the motion. She doubted that she looked marvelous, but she knew how much difference a hot shower and clean clothes could make after a long night of work. Eric wouldn't sleep, she knew, but he'd shower, shave and change and eat, and return feeling renewed, and she needed him feeling renewed, because there would be no rest until they knew everything there was to know about Sandra Phillips, Ellie Litton, and Millicent Cartcher. And until they found out who Sandy and Ellie and Millie had in common— because Gianna was convinced that the three women were lured to the Washington, D.C. area by the same person. Knowing who that was would lead them to the identities of the three Jane Does, the other victims.

Gianna's phone rang, her private line, and she snatched it up, the relief in her voice audible at the sound of Mimi's voice, exhausted though it was. She'd had to fly into Baltimore-Washington International Airport, via Atlanta, in order to arrive in time for work. She would, she said, tell Gianna all about it later. Unless, of course, she planned to work all night again. Gianna assured her that was not the case, and after agreeing where and when they'd meet later that evening, Gianna hung up feeling truly renewed. She had not wanted to admit to herself how really worried she'd been about Mimi. She wasn't surprised that Mimi's cell phone was either turned off or that the battery was dead— Mimi hated the telephone. She spent ninety percent of her working life on the phone, and as little time as possible on it when not working. But she was surprised that Mimi wouldn't have known how worried she'd be.

"Come in!" she snapped at whoever was knocking on her door as she looked at her watch. She stood up as the door opened and Alice Long entered. "I'm on my way down, Alice," she said.

"I need a moment, Lieutenant, if you don't mind."

Gianna waved her in and into the chair beside her desk, and sat back down, instantly on alert. "What is it, Alice?"

"One of those Jane Does, one of the Black women. I may have met her. I was reading through the autopsy reports this morning, and there's mention of a kind of birth mark on one the women. A misshapen ear..."

"I recall that," Gianna said slowly, "though didn't the ME call it more of a birth defect?" she asked, recalling the the particulars of that autopsy report and waiting for confirmation or clarification.

Alice didn't respond immediately, obviously very shaken by what she had discovered. It was one thing to be a cop, to be an observer and a chronicler of society's evils; but it was something else entirely to have a personal relationship with that evil. To find familiarity within the uncensored and graphic language of an autopsy report would be disconcerting, to say the least. "I suppose that's really what it was," she replied quietly, the soft edges of her Southern accent the perfect resting place for the sorrow she obviously felt. "She'd had it cosmetically repaired, but if you looked real close, you could tell it wasn't a normal ear. But you know the funny thing? Nobody would have noticed if she hadn't called attention to it herself, either by telling people about it, or by trying to hide it. I guess when you live with a thing, it's always noticeable to you."

Gianna allowed a moment for the weight of Alice's words to settle before asking, "What was her name, Alice? Do you remember? Do you recall anything else about her? Where she lived?"

"I only was in her company twice. I remember she was very nice and very shy, not really comfortable in a large group of people, even if she did know most of them. But very nice, with a sweet smile. A gentle person. And she always sat at a table with her face resting on her hand. So she could cover up her ear."

"Alice..."

"I met her because she was from near my hometown. There's a group of us that keep in touch with the roots, so to speak, men and women, all ages. We laugh about how many queers that rich South Carolina soil produced. Most of us have been up here for years, came up to go to college or to the military and stayed, but Mabel had just gotten here. That was her name: Mabel. I've been wracking my brain trying to come up with a last name, but I can't remember it. I'll call some of the others and see if anybody knows, if you want me to. They'll want to know, since a couple of 'em felt like they had to keep watch out for her."

Gianna walked around her desk to stand beside Alice, whose dark, lovely eyes were swimming with tears that Gianna knew the other cop would not let fall. "Somebody else can make those calls, Alice," she said gently, placing a hand on the other woman's shoulder.

A tremor coursed through Alice's body. Gianna felt it and resisted the impulse to move her hand. Instead, she applied gentle pressure, and Alice calmed almost immediately. "I'll do it, Lieutenant. They wouldn't talk about a home girl to a stranger. Especially somebody like Mabel."

"What do you mean, 'especially somebody like Mabel'? What about her?"

All of the emotion Alice had worked to contain beneath the veneer of professionalism escaped in a sob of pure frustration. "She was a mess, Lieutenant! All she talked about was how much she hated that ear, and how much she hated that she was getting older, and how much she hated that she was heavy, and how she'd wasted her whole life, stuck in some country South Carolina town, waiting for somebody to love. She hadn't had very much experience, if you know what I mean. She came up here because of some woman she hooked up with in one of those internet chat rooms. Hadn't met the woman in person but once, and hadn't ever had sex with her. But she was in love! We tried to reason with her, but she wouldn't listen. Said we'd understand when we were all old and fat like she was. When we were faced with a last chance at love. That's what she called it, Lieutenant: A last chance at love. Isn't that the saddest, most pitiful, craziest thing you ever heard?"

Sad and crazy and pitiful, perhaps, Gianna thought, and almost certainly deadly.

"You were supposed to be on R and R, Patterson, not digging up murders. And how did you get murder out of this anyway?" Tyler was not as excited as Mimi about the possibility that Millicent Cartcher and Ellie Litton were the tip of a very deep and dangerous iceberg. Her discovery that morning, sitting at her desk drinking juice and catching up on a week's worth of papers, that Ellie Litton had been found murdered on the grounds of the Lincoln Memorial was galvanizing; and while she dreaded having to call Sue and Kate with the news, and their friend, Sarah, who'd grown up with the murdered woman, the sense that she was on the brink of a major story was working its usual magic on her.

"Surely you see the potential here, Tyler." They were huddled at their usual spot in the hallway near the water cooler, she trying to capture his attention, he trying to escape back to his desk.

"All you've got is two dead women, Patterson--"

"Two dead *lesbians,* Tyler--"

"Which means diddly. Lesbians get offed in this sick society like every other segment of the population, there being plenty of equal opportunity killers." He stalked off and left her standing beside the water cooler.

She returned to her desk and began sorting through the stack of mail that had accumulated during the week she was away, but her focus wandered until she accepted that delaying the inevitable would not make it more palatable. She considered whether to call Sue or Kate, since at this time of day she couldn't speak to them both simultaneously. "Sure you can, Patterson." The voice of disdain spoke to her and she made a conference call, getting both women on the line. Their grief was deep, mitigated only by their gratitude for Mimi's immediate response. They brushed off her insistence that she'd done nothing more than read a week's worth of newspapers that morning by noting that she cared enough to pay attention when they expressed concern about their missing friend. That was more than they'd expected, and they were grateful. If Mimi wouldn't mind, they'd appreciate her keeping them apprised of the results of the police investigation. She promised that she would, hung up, grabbed her purse, and rushed out of the newsroom.

The young parking lot attendant muttered something that probably was profanity in Hindi when she showed up to claim her car. She'd been in the lot for only about three hours and he had expected her to be there for at least six more, so her car was against the wall, with four others in front of it. She gave him a nonchalant wave, signaling that she was in no hurry, and propped her butt on one of the concrete stanchions used to separate the monthly parkers from the daily cars. She immediately felt the cold through her gabardine slacks and she shivered. She looked up at the sky. The pewter-colored clouds hung low and looked full. Winter was at hand. She raised the collar on her jacket as a light wind pushed through the parking lot and wished that she'd dressed more warmly. Then she remembered that these were the clothes she'd worn home from Florida. No wonder she was cold; she was dressed for November in Florida, not November in D.C.

She stood up, stuffed her hands into her pockets, and paced back and forth until the attendant brought her car. She apologized, gave him five dollars for his trouble, and roared out of the lot and into the mid-morning traffic, the new engine in the thirty-five year old Karmann Ghia easily allowing her to keep pace with the newer stuff on the road. Almost of its own volition, the car headed east, across the northern edge of town toward the Washington Women's Gym.

She thought of Kate as she sat in traffic, watching a light turn yellow and then red for the third time, and wondered if there ever would come a time when she would miss spending a quarter of an hour to traverse a single block. Perhaps if she had no particular place to be and no particular time to be there, it wouldn't matter how long it took. As it was, however, she was stealing time from the paper; and though she knew it was time well-spent, she didn't want to waste the precious minutes sitting still, watching the light change. She should have, she thought, told the newsroom AA that she was going to be out for a while, but she'd checked in with her editor. Anyway, she wouldn't be able to write a word in the condition she was in. And since she couldn't go home and go to bed, a workout and a sauna would be the next most restorative thing she could do.

Once she cleared the downtown gridlock, the cross-town journey was a pleasant one. She always enjoyed how, as the topography changed, so did the city's energy, from downtown's edgy pretentiousness to the collegiate atmosphere of Brookland near Catholic and Gallaudet Universities to the laid back artsy feel of the northeast warehouse district, her ultimate destination. Because Washington was a relatively small city— relative to New York or Chicago or Los Angeles or Philadelphia or Atlanta-- traversing it was neither difficult nor particularly time consuming, even given the ever increasing traffic. And because of its low-to-the-ground nature, it was possible to see quite a bit of the city on a northwest-to-northeast trip. Federal law forbade any structure from being taller than the Washington Monument; so while the city had achieved a certain horizontal density, tall buildings didn't obliterate large chunks of the sight line. Thus, in addition to noticing that pedestrians were huddled into their coats and striding with purpose toward their destinations, signaling winter's arrival, Mimi noticed also that Grand Opening sales were in progress in two new clothing boutiques and an electronics store, and that gasoline prices hadn't dropped as low as predicted. She noticed how many of the trees were in full fall regalia, how bold their reds and oranges and yellows appeared against the dull, grey sky, and she was glad she was here in D.C. and not in Florida where it was warm and sunny and the foliage was tropical and green.

Once inside the gym she hurried to her locker and

changed into tights and an exercise bra. She was rummaging around in her gym bag in search of an errant sock when three sweat-drenched, novice body builders burst noisily into the locker room. She didn't know any of them well enough to speak to, though she'd noticed them in the last couple of months. She'd been a regular at this gym for half a dozen years now, and until recently, afternoons by unspoken agreement belonged to the committed, serious body builders. The surging interest in physical health and well-being meant that more women now used the gym at all hours, which didn't bother Mimi; the only thing that bothered her was having to wait to use the equipment, and that had never happened during the afternoon. Yet. She found her sock and sat on the bench to put them on, aware of the conversation between the other women, but not really listening. Until she heard the words, "old dykes looking for love." She tuned in to the conversation.

"You better watch your mouth, Girl. One day you're gonna be the old dyke somebody's making fun of."

"I might get old, but I won't be saggy and out of shape like them! And they got the nerve to have on spandex."

"You got nerve criticizing those women like that."

"Don't forget she likes her women old."

"I like my women *mature*, because mature women don't say the kind of stupid things like you just did."

"Yeah, they just look stupid, stuffing their fat bodies into spandex."

Mimi, disgusted, had heard enough. She tied her shoes, slammed her locker door shut, and tried to put as much distance as quickly as possible between herself and people she hoped she'd never have to have direct contact with. She all but ran to the row of treadmills, stepped onto her favorite machine, and in less than a minute was running at full speed. She began to relax as she found her stride and her rhythm, and, taking a look around, she spied the women that no doubt had been the topic of such ugly conversation in the locker room. There were four of them, women

88

she guessed were in their fifties, and none deserving of the awful assessment she'd overheard just moments earlier. They were alternating sets on the leg machines— presses, curls, squats and lifts. They worked slowly but methodically, getting the most out of each set of repetitions, though from a distance it seemed that the woman on the leg curl machine was struggling with too much weight. And at that precise moment, she let out a little squeal and dropped the bar. The weight bars clanged down hard, making a resonant, crashing sound. Mimi leapt off the treadmill mid-stride and reached the group of women at the same pace she'd been running.

"Are you all right?" she asked the woman seated on the leg curl machine, surmising from the grimace on her face what the answer would be.

"I think I pulled something," the woman said.

"Can you stand up?" Mimi asked, and stood aside while offering a hand of assistance as the woman slid herself sideways in the seat and then hopped to the floor. She limped for a few steps, then straightened and steadied.

"I think it's OK. Thanks for charging to the rescue." She smiled and stuck out her hand. "I'm Phyllis, and these are my friends." She introduced them one by one: June, Evie, Dot— and they all shook hands. "How long have you been coming here?" Phyllis asked once the pleasantries were out of the way.

"A few years," Mimi replied.

"We can tell," Evie responded. "You're in absolutely wonderful shape."

Mimi ignored the meaning beneath the words and the accompanying assessing look. "Do you have a trainer here?"

They all shook their heads, and June asked, "Why? Do we need one?"

"It seemed that you were trying to lift too much weight. That's the quickest way to get hurt."

"We're trying to lose some weight and we thought the best and fastest way to do that would be to put more weight on

89

the machine," Phyllis said.

Mimi shook her head. "The opposite is true. Less weight and more reps. That'll burn the calories faster." She leaned across the machine, pulled the pin in the stack of weights and replaced it in a higher plate. "Try it now," she said to Phyllis, and helped her into the seat. Phyllis grasped the hand rails, stuck her feet beneath the padded bar, and lifted. Up and down and up and down, slowly and methodically and properly.

Phyllis nodded. "That's better. It doesn't feel like I'm straining."

"And it shouldn't feel that way," Mimi said.

"What about no pain, no gain?" Evie asked.

"Grossly overrated as a concept," Mimi replied. "What could you possibly gain by hurting yourself on a regular basis?"

"A body like yours," June shot back at her, looking her up and down. "You can't tell me you manage to look like that by taking it slow and easy."

"I could take it slow and easy with her," Evie said.

Mimi ignored Evie, kept eye contact with Phyllis. "I've been coming here three or four times a week for five or six years," she said, "no secrets, no miracles."

"How about fewer birthdays?" asked Dot, who'd been quiet up to that point. "It makes a difference that you're younger than we are."

Mimi shook her head. "Not a bit." Four pairs of eyes gave her an incredulous look and she could all but see the sarcasm dripping.

"Easy for you to say," Evie said, and the sarcasm dripped. "Have you even had your fortieth birthday yet?"

Not willing to be drawn into that conversation, Mimi smiled. "Three or four days a week, continuously increasing the number of reps, and maybe every few months increasing the amount of weight is the way to burn calories, if that's what you're after. It was nice meeting all of you. See you tomorrow?" she said with raised eyebrows, and, with a wave, returned to her treadmill.

As she departed, she heard suppressed giggles and one loud guffaw, which sounded exactly like Sue, and Mimi wondered whether any of them were looking for love, whether one of them was a reluctant roommate, and why she'd never before noticed the fifty-something women in the gym.

"Because you're supposed to be watching your own form— and occasionally mine— not those of other women, that's why you never noticed." Gianna replied lazily, caressing Mimi's right nipple.

"I know, but a couple of them had forms worth noticing, especially the one named--" Mimi didn't get the name out because Gianna claimed her mouth in a bruising kiss, and it was some time before she could return to the subject. "You wouldn't by any chance be jealous, would you?"

"Of course I am," Gianna replied matter-of-factly if distractedly, as she now was attending to Mimi's left nipple. "And what's the name of this older woman I now have to worry about? And what was it about her form that got your attention?"

"Well, I'm flattered. I'll take a generous helping of jealousy after being so totally and thoroughly ignored."

Gianna released the nipple she was massaging and raised herself on her right elbow to gaze down into Mimi's face. The glow cast by the flickering of the candles burning on the bedside tables highlighted the chocolate brown skin recently burnished by the Florida sun, even as it accentuated the fatigue that Gianna could see in her eyes. And the seriousness. "You think I've been ignoring you?"

"I tried to talk to you three different times when I was in Florida, and you couldn't take two minutes to talk to me."

"Mimi, I was buried under--"

"I know you're busy, Gianna. I know how hard you work, and I don't often ask for your time. But when I do, I don't think it's asking too much for you to stop and give me two minutes, unless you're actually processing a dead body or chasing a perp."

91

Gianna peered deeply into Mimi's eyes, her clear hazel ones finding both love and reproach in the dark brown ones. "Shouldn't we talk about this another time?"

Mimi pushed Gianna away and sat up. "You do this all the time. Why can't you talk right now?"

"I do what all the time? And we can talk about it now if you want to. I just thought you looked tired and that you should get a good sleep tonight."

"But we could make love for another two hours and you wouldn't worry about whether I was getting enough sleep." Mimi's statement was accusatory and flat, emotionless.

Gianna sat up, too, and turned to face Mimi. "What's bothering you?"

"That we don't talk."

"We talk all the time!"

"About everything but what we spend ninety percent of our waking hours doing: our jobs. You wouldn't talk to me when I called because you didn't want to have to tell me what's going on with the murders of older lesbians."

Gianna concealed and controlled the anger and frustration that so quickly welled up inside of her. How the hell did Mimi always know about her investigations? And *why* the hell was she always sniffing along the same trail? "You know I can't talk about my cases, Mimi, with anyone. Not just you."

"And I'm not asking you to talk about your cases specifically, Gianna. I'm asking you to tell me what you think and feel." She held up a hand to halt Gianna's protest. "For example, what would be wrong with saying something like, 'I'm really worried about these murders?' I know better than to ask you about specifics, but at least I'd have some sense of what you were coping with, and what I should expect of you. For example, I wouldn't have had to be so worried about getting back last night to be with you had I known how intensely you were working this case. I'd have slept later, had a big brunch, and not had to suffer being trapped in a parking lot by a truck full of drunken

Irishmen. Which is why I missed my plane, by the way."

"Drunken Irishmen," Gianna snapped. "What drunken Irishmen? Where?"

Mimi gave her a wary look. "In the parking lot of the cafe where I ate breakfast Sunday before I left Florida. Why? What's your interest in drunken Irishmen?"

Gianna hopped out of bed, ran around to Mimi's side and stood over her. "Tell me, Mimi, please!"

"Tell me why you want to know."

"That's blackmail!"

"Call it what you like, but I'm not giving up any info without a reason."

Gianna scowled, shivered, and hopped back into bed, snuggled against Mimi, and told her about the Irish, the guns, and the Ganja. Then Mimi told her how she'd left Sue and Kate's early Sunday morning and stopped to have breakfast at a waterfront cafe before heading to the airport. When she returned to her car, she found herself hemmed in by a blue panel van that wouldn't start. Meaningful conversation with the van's driver failed because he was blind drunk, even at so early an hour, as were his two passengers. The only thing she could ascertain through the alcohol haze and the thick brogues was that the truck wouldn't start. She got the restaurant manager involved. She called a tow truck. By the time the truck arrived to tow the van, it was too late for Mimi to make her flight. "But now that I'm remembering it, I remember thinking that if I were home, here in D.C., I'd jot down the license plate number of that van and report the driver."

"Why?" Gianna asked.

"Because it was illegal. It had a commercial tag on the front and a passenger tag on the rear."

"Do you recall the plate numbers?" And when Mimi shook her head, she demanded as full a description as Mimi could recall of the men in the truck and of the truck itself.

"You really think it's them?"

"Yeah," Gianna said, "I do. It fits. They can buy guns all day long in Georgia and Florida and South Carolina, and not have to worry that the license plates would be noticed. But closer to home, in North Carolina and Virginia, where people know what D.C. tags are like, they'd have a problem." She reached for the phone. "I wish I knew the chief's home phone number," she muttered, punching buttons.

"I know it," Mimi said casually, "but who're you calling if not the chief?"

Gianna punched off the phone and looked at Mimi. "You really know the chief's private home telephone number?"

"Sure," Mimi said as if talking to a new arrival to the planet, and she rattled it off as Gianna punched the buttons, all the while muttering to herself. Mimi got up and went to the bathroom, and when she returned, Gianna was sitting in the middle of the bed with the covers up around her shoulders, a bemused look on her face.

"So," she said.

"So what?" Mimi asked, crawling into bed and under the covers, plastering her body next to Gianna's.

"Don't you want to know what the chief said, and don't you want to know how we're going to find the Irish and the guns?"

Mimi yawned and shook her head. "No, I don't. I don't care about the Irish and their guns, or about the Jamaicans. I just want to go to sleep."

"Well," Gianna said, snuggling against her, "I want to know the name of that woman you were ogling in the gym, and what aspect of her form you found so intriguing, and whether I need to spend extra time in the gym working on that aspect.."

Mimi yawned again and mumbled something Gianna couldn't hear but which sounded like "breasts." It was a while longer before she was able to just go to sleep.

94

CHAPTER SEVEN

The casual observer would not have believed that Sandra Phillips had lived in D.C. barely three weeks. The third floor of the bay front house that was her new home possessed that well-cared for, lived-in look: pictures, curtains, blinds, shutters and clothes neatly hung; books, video tapes and compact discs neatly shelved. The refrigerator and cabinets were well-stocked, the dishes in the dishwasher were clean. The cable guide and the remote were in a basket of magazines beside the easy chair that faced the television across the living room. The small stack of cardboard boxes, cut and flattened and tied and ready for the recycling bin, might suggest a lack of longevity; but to the practiced eye, it was the newness of everything that bore witness to the truth of Sandra Phillips's tenancy. Everything— furniture, clothes, dishes, the paintings on the wall, the rugs on the hardwood floors— was just-out-of-the-carton new. Only the objects in the room that Sandra Phillips used as an office were well-used and seasoned, as if they had belonged to her in a previous life. Even the paintings in the hallway leading up to her third-floor walk-up, and the mat at her door, screamed their newness. As did the bulb in the fixture above the door, which was burning a full two hundred and fifty watts when the women of the Hate Crimes Unit arrived to begin their investigation. "Security conscious, paranoid, or just scared to death to be in the big city?" Cassie Ali wondered aloud as she blinked at the light that was blinding even in broad daylight.

"All of the above," Alice Long had replied when they finally threw the third dead bolt and entered the immaculate apartment.

"And a neat freak, "Linda Lopez murmured as she strolled about the apartment, scrutinizing and assessing. "The woman hasn't been here in two days and there's not a speck of dust anywhere, not even in a corner. Even the dust knows better than to show up in here."

Gianna didn't say anything, but everything she saw caused her to grow more and more uneasy. They all had pulled on latex gloves upon entering the building, and aside from the most cursory of checks, wouldn't disturb the premises until the crime scene investigators finished their work. But Gianna wanted— desperately needed— to find some clue as to who Sandy Phillips was, some bit or piece of information or knowledge that would explain her move to D.C., her presence at *The Bayou* the night she was killed, the reason for her departure from the norm of her previous existence. Gianna's gaze went everywhere, and though Sandy Phillips's apartment was fully furnished, it may as well have been as empty as Ellie Litton's town house was when they finally received permission to search it, so devoid of personality was this place.

Without a word spoken among them, Alice turned down the hallway to the bedroom, Linda crossed the living room into the kitchen, Cassie crossed to the bookshelves in the living room and stood, head thrown back, to read up at the neatly aligned spines, and Gianna invaded the only space that spoke Sandy Phillips's name.

The room at the rear of the apartment that Dr. Sandra Phillips had set up as an office overlooked the backyard terrace that all the residents of the house shared, and it was here, Gianna believed, that any vestiges of the old Sandy Phillips would remain, if indeed any did. She stood in the doorway of the room, hoping for a sense of the woman who had lived here so briefly.

An L-shaped desk was in front of the windows, and on it, all the tools expected of a 21st century academic: computer and monitor, printer, fax machine, scanner. A bookshelf adjacent to the desk was filled with academic-looking books and books were stacked in neat piles on the floor beside the desk and on top of it. The heavy drapes at the windows were closed, suggesting several things to Gianna: that the upstate New York native knew very well how to insulate against the cold; that she knew she'd spend a lot of time at this desk, and would need the barrier against the winter winds just beginning to blow; that Alice and Linda and Cassie were right on in their assessment of Sandy Phillips's proclivity toward paranoia and the heavy drapes certainly would obliterate the outside world.

The doorbell sounded, followed seconds later by voices, and Gianna returned to the living room. The landlord, who'd been called and who had agreed to meet them at the apartment, confirmed their impressions of Sandra Phillips. Jared Taylor was his name, and he began by saying that Sandra Phillips was a "dreamboat" of a tenant. Jared was eighty-two years old and looked like Ray Bradbury. He was tiny, the way older people sometimes are, but with not the slightest hint of frailty. His blue eyes sparkled with mischief like a child's despite the bushy white eyebrows above them, but they also held a wealth of wisdom, and the cadence of his voice was slightly Southern. He had raised his family in this house when it was a single family residence, but when his children grew up and moved away and when his wife had a stroke, he converted the three-story building into three flats and moved with his wife to an assisted living complex in Montgomery County.

All of his tenants, he said, were long term, and he had expected that Sandra Phillips would be, too. The top floor became vacant when the woman who'd lived there for a decade and worked for the State Department got a promotion and moved to Europe. Jared rented only to "mature, professional women," he said, because they were more responsible than any other group of people. He'd had a total of three conversations with Sandra Phillips: one on the telephone, and two in person, the second when she moved in two weeks ago. He described her as polite, articulate, and "a little bit young for her age."

"What does that mean, Mr. Taylor?" Alice Long asked. Cassie wrote his reply in her notebook.

"According to her application and her tax returns, she was

97

fifty-six years old, but when you met her in person, you had the feeling she hadn't seen any more of life than a sheltered child. She said she was glad the place was on the top floor, and she asked me to install a third security lock, and the first day she put in that million-watt bulb. I told her it was safe, that we hadn't ever had in trouble in this building, and I've owned it for almost fifty years. But she said no place was safe, and that nobody could be too careful." He took a deep breath. "I can't tell you how sorry I am about what happened to Dr. Phillips, but I can tell you I'm grateful that it didn't happen to her in this building. I told her the truth when I said there's never been any trouble in this building or in this block."

"She lived in upstate New York, Mr. Taylor," Alice said, bringing the old man back from his mental musings. "How'd she find out about your place?"

Jared Taylor's smile was almost smug. "I only advertise in professional journals. My youngest daughter taught me that one. Professor Phillips saw my ad in the social workers journal. I forget what it's called..."

The old man was on a roll and Gianna had to leave in a few minutes, so as much as she regretted having to do it, she cut him off. "Did she have any visitors that you know of? Or receive any mail or packages that you're aware of?"

He shook his head. "I got the feeling she didn't know anybody here at all. And to tell you the truth, I was surprised that she had the gumption to pick up and move all the way down here. I'm telling you, she struck me as a sheltered type of person. Smart as a whip— you could tell by talking to her that she was smart— and she was pretty as a picture. But all she knew came from books, you know what I mean? Not from life. Now that Dr. Jenkins who lived here, the one who went to Europe? Now she was the adventuresome sort."

Gianna cut in again to ask whether Sandy Phillips had used a professional moving company or whether her move had been a do-it-yourself operation, and Jared cut her a big, wide grin

98

and threw in a knowing wink and Gianna had to work not to return the gestures in kind. Then he explained that Sandra Phillips had arrived driving her brand new Cadillac and towing "one of those little U-Haul trailers. Nothing in it but her desk and chair and computer stuff and all those books. She paid the guys next door a hundred bucks to unload it for her. All the furniture came the next day from a local store, not some place in New York, and I thought that was kind of unusual."

Gianna's cell phone rang and she excused herself, returning to Sandy Phillips's office to answer it and leaving Cassie, Alice and Linda to finish with Jared Taylor. She switched gears completely to listen to Eric update her on the status of the panel van Mimi had told her about. She looked at her watch. She had a meeting with the chief in forty minutes. She was pressing her luck by being with Cassie, Alice and Linda in Sandra Phillips's apartment, but the chief was so pleased that she'd found the Irish guns she felt safe taking a step on the wild side. But only a step. She needed to get back to the office. She told Eric to meet her there and punched off the phone.

She took a quick look through the papers on the desk and opened all the drawers. Nothing there she wouldn't expect to find. Then she realized that one thing she would expect to find was missing: a telephone. The only phone was the one that was part of the fax machine.

She picked up the handset with her thumb and index finger and held it to her ear. Dead. She carefully lifted the machine, looking for its connections to the computer tower. All the wires dangled freely. Then she took a close look at the computer. She was no technocrat but she knew hi tech when she saw it, and Sandy Phillips's computer set-up was the Cadillac. Just like her car, big, new, the top of the line. She recalled from the ME's report on Ellie Litton the fact that every article of clothing she wore was brand new, even her underwear. A killer with a "new" fetish? But that wouldn't explain why the computer wasn't hooked up or why there was no telephone. The woman had been here for three weeks. She had to have talked on the phone, to have used her computer, to have checked her e-mail.

Then Gianna backed away from the desk and scrutinized the area. Something about it had bothered her earlier, before Jared Taylor arrived. She studied the scene before her. The stacks of books on the floor beside the desk and on top of the desk. Yes, the piles were neat, but not, she thought, truly reflective of who Sandra Phillips seemed to be. A neat freak, Linda had called her. Paranoid and obsessive about her possessions and surroundings. Sandra Phillips would not have piles of books on the floor or on the desk, no matter how neatly they were stacked. Gianna knelt down and read the lettering on the book spines on the floor, then rose to read those on the desk. Text books and theses and sociological studies of varying kinds. The same kind of things that were on the shelves. She looked at her watch again, took a last look around the room, and sped out. She thanked Jared Taylor for his help and began to explain that the crime scene investigators would want to take his fingerprints.

"Oh, I know all about that," he said sagely. "That's to eliminate me as a suspect when they find my prints all over the place."

"I wish all witnesses could take lessons from you, Mr. Taylor," Gianna said shaking his hand. She tossed a backhanded salute to her Team and all but ran down the steps and out the front door.

She shivered at the blast of cold air that met her. She hadn't been aware of being too warm inside the apartment. "Maybe I'm getting old and my blood's thinning," she mused, and heard her mother's voice saying that exact thing as clearly as if she were in the car with her. The memory warmed her faster than the car's heater. She reached for the car's mobile phone, punched in the number of her favorite deli, and ordered half a dozen sandwiches. She was certain that Eric, Tim, Bobby and Tony hadn't eaten; and even if they had, she was certain they'd eat again without hesitation. And she was ravenous. She'd barely

100

replaced the receiver when the cell phone in her purse rang. She grabbed it, flipped it open, listened for several seconds, and couldn't stop the curse that rose up and out.

"I'll be right there." She closed the phone, took a hurried look into the rear view mirror, and made a U-turn. Then she called the chief and explained why she wouldn't be meeting with him in the next half an hour as scheduled and, mercifully, he gave her no grief. He agreed to let Eric brief him and extracted a promise from her that she'd see him before the end of the day. She hung up the phone, activated lights and siren, and was back in front of Jared Taylor's house in a few minutes.

The white, unmarked big rig was at the curb. Gianna pulled to a stop at its front bumper and was hanging her badge on her jacket pocket when she leaped out of the car. With her right hand, she reached under her left arm as she ran up the walkway to the house. The door swung out just as she reached the bottom step, and she backpedaled out of the way of the man who tumbled down the steps and sprawled face down on the ground, Alice Long close behind. She straddled him, grabbed one arm and then the other, and handcuffed the snarling, cursing fellow before giving him a hard smack to the back of the head with the open palm of her hand, and the admonition to shut his nasty mouth before she shut it for him. Then she noticed Gianna.

"Lieutenant," she said in her soft voice that registered no hint of the exertion she'd just endured. "I don't know yet what all this ol' boy is gonna be charged with, but assault on a police officer is gonna be the first item on the list." She got to her feet and cradled her mid-section with a grimace. "He sucker-punched me. I should've seen it coming. Must be getting slow in my old age."

Gianna stepped over to the prone man who still was muttering under his breath and leaned toward his face. "Stand up, sir."

"Fuck you bitch," the man mumbled without conviction.

"You don't want me to ask you again," Gianna said, and

101

the man looked into her eyes and struggled to a sitting position. "All the way up," Gianna said.

"You wanna tell me what this shit is all about?" the man whined as he got to his feet. "I'm here just trying to do my job and all of a sudden I got cop bitches in my face, 'bout to cost me a whole bunch of money."

"If you use that word one more time, you're going to spend the night in a place where it takes on a completely different meaning," Gianna said, and watched with satisfaction as she saw that he understood her meaning. "What is your name and who sent you to clean out this apartment?"

Raul Lozano was the truck driver's name. He was in his forties, about six feet tall, and had the wiry, muscular build of one who used his body in his work. His hair was black and curly and shot through with silver, as was his thick mustache, and his bad attitude dried up and blew away like tumbleweeds in the desert when he finally understood that big trouble was in his face, along with the cops, and that the situation could cost him much more than mere money. He started shaking his head, frustrated by his inability to use his hands. "I'm not here to 'clean out' no apartment! I got hired to move somebody. I got the paperwork in the cab."

"Who hired you?"

Lozano shrugged. "Some company. Done lotsa jobs for 'em the last couple years. I move people whose jobs move them."

"I want a name, Mr. Lozano, and I want it now."

"I don't know nobody's name. It's just another job."

"Get the paperwork out of the truck." Gianna gave Alice a look and she stepped behind Lozano and removed his handcuffs. When the truck driver looked back at Gianna, her Glock was in her hand and pointed at him. "If you give me a reason, Mr. Lozano, I'll shoot you, and that's a promise, not a threat."

Lozano rubbed his wrists and shook his head in disbelief. "I won't, lady. I ain't no criminal, for Christ's sake, I'm a truck driver."

102

"Then why'd you punch me?" Alice, obviously still in pain, was not inclined to accept Lozano's declaration as gospel. "That's the kind of thing criminals do, and you did it real easy, like it was something you'd done before."

"'Cause you made me mad, lady, jumpin' in my face like that, when all I did was knock on the goddamn door! That was just reflexes acting, that's all, and that's the truth. I don't go around punching people, 'specially girls."

"In that case, you're lucky all I did was throw you down the stairs. I could've shot you. And I haven't been a girl in twenty years."

Lozano's eyes widened but instead of speaking, he turned away from them and ambled over to his truck. They followed him across the well-trimmed, winter brown lawn to the curb and the truck. He hoisted his right foot up to the big rig's step, gripped the hand rail, and swung up with the ease of habit. When he opened the truck's door, Gianna told him to leave it open, and to leave his feet visible in the door frame. When he backed down to the ground, a manila file folder in his hand, and turned around, he gasped at the sight of two gun barrels pointed at him, and backed into the truck's tire. "What the hell do y'all think I did?"

Gianna reached for the folder without speaking.

"Do you want him handcuffed, Boss?" Alice asked.

"Not if he behaves himself," Gianna answered, then turned to the truck driver. "You're going to be here for a while, Mr. Lozano, so relax." She holstered her gun and walked away, reading the papers in Lozano's file. The trucker struggled for composure. He lit a cigarette and watched Alice Long watch him. It was getting colder; the wind blew icy and, given their proximity to the Potomac, damp. Alice, in wool slacks, jacket and sweater, was almost comfortable. Raul Lozano, in jeans and a long-sleeved denim shirt, was not. He blew on his hands and shivered. "Can I get my jacket outta the cab?"

Alice nodded and he climbed up and back out in a matter of seconds, a Baltimore Orioles cap fitting snugly on his head. He slipped into a fleece-lined parka, which he zipped all the way up. Then he lit another cigarette and smoked in silence while Alice watched him, her face a calm, unreadable mask. Both were glad when Gianna returned, the manila folder tucked under her arm. She stepped in close to Lozano.

"The woman who lived here, Sandra Phillips, was murdered, so despite what it says in these papers, she's not being transferred to a new job in Texas. Do you hear and understand what I'm telling you, Mr. Lozano?"

He did. He dropped his cigarette, crossed himself, and looked from Gianna to Alice and back to Gianna. "I don't know nothing but what's in those papers, I swear to God I don't! *Oh, Madre de Dios, yo no soy un asesino*"

"Mr. Lozano," Gianna said in her calm tone. He looked again into her clear hazel eyes, and again found a reason to listen, and to believe. "At the moment, I'm inclined to take your word for your presence here, but we will need your full cooperation. Do you understand me and are you prepared to cooperate?"

"*Si, senora, yo entiendo.*"

"It's Lieutenant, Mr. Lozano, and unfortunately, your English is a lot better than my Spanish, OK?"

And when he almost smiled and nodded, she asked whether he'd planned to carry Sandra Phillips's belongings out to the truck by himself. This time he smiled broadly and answered that he came today, after unloading a job nearby, to assess how long this job would take and how many men he would need. He would arrange to have the requisite number of workers here tomorrow morning at dawn to begin packing and wrapping.

"Then we have until tomorrow morning at dawn, Mr. Lozano, to understand what's happening here and to decide what we're going to do about it."

Beverly was looking at her like she was a new species that hadn't yet been classified. "What?" Mimi said in response to the look that was beginning to feel uncomfortable.

104

"What, indeed," Beverly replied, still giving Mimi that look and enjoying Mimi's discomfort.

Because it was a new one Mimi didn't know exactly what it meant and therefore didn't know exactly how to respond, though she had an idea. Their break-up more than three years earlier had been unpleasant in the extreme due primarily to Mimi's behavior. Because of that, it had taken some time and lots of work to rebuild the friendship between them; and because they'd worked so hard, the friendship was solid, built on love and trust and forgiveness. If only they'd done all that work *before* they'd broken up.

Mimi gave Bev a look of her own— one both appraising and appreciative. Beverly was one of those women who became more beautiful as she aged. The long, thick dreadlocks that were gathered and held by a brightly colored cloth were streaked with silver and the laugh lines at the corners of her mouth were deep and sensuous. And though amply endowed of bust and butt, Mimi always was captivated by Bev's eyes. They were deep-set and dark and liquid and they revealed exactly what was in Bev's head and heart. Right now they were questioning Mimi's presence and motives with equal parts warmth, love and skepticism.

"It's a weird question, I know."

"Mimi, it's more than just weird, it's so far removed from what I've come to expect from you that I'm having a hard time taking it seriously. Yet, I know you must be serious because you wouldn't interrupt my work otherwise."

Beverly Connors had spent fifteen years as a public school guidance counselor. Frustrated by and fed up with the school system, she'd completed her doctorate in clinical social work and a year and a half ago had set up shop with three other therapists in a beautifully renovated town house in a raggedy, run-down, dangerous neighborhood whose residents needed all the guidance, counseling, and intervention they could get. Most of them were low level government, hospital, and association employees who didn't earn enough money to pay rent and buy groceries with the same paycheck, but whose jobs provided the kind of insurance that bought them and their children an hour a week at Midtown Psychotherapy Associates.

"No, I wouldn't, and I truly appreciate your making time for me."

Bev snorted in a truly unladylike fashion. "I didn't make time for you; I accepted a bribe, Miss Patterson." And she gave Mimi the leering, lecherous grin that still could make her insides lurch. Mimi walked around the desk and presented Bev with a shopping bag that contained all of her favorite foods from an Ethiopian restaurant on 18th Street in Adams-Morgan that was a favorite.

Bev peeked into the bag and made yummy sounds. "Get out your pad and pencil, Girl, you've bought yourself a full hour's worth of everything I know about what happens in the bodies and psyches of women over fifty. But first, Mimi, you really must tell me why you're asking. This isn't the kind of thing you do or care about."

"It's so not the kind of thing I do that I'm still not sure exactly what it is I'm doing, but I'm caring more about it every day," Mimi said, and proceeded to tell Beverly everything that had ignited and then fueled her interest in what was shaping up to be more than just a newspaper story about a couple of murdered lesbians, though she told her the little that she knew about the deaths of Millicent Cartcher and Ellie Litton. And she told her about the ugly conversation she'd overheard in the locker room at the gym, and about the women willing to hurt themselves on gym equipment in order to lose a few pounds and about their defiant defense of their actions, and about the sexless union between Kate and Sue and the hopeless tone of Sue's rationale for remaining in an unhappy union.

"I've read dozens of articles by and about baby boomers and the over-fifty set, and I'm left with the impression that they're essentially healthy, upbeat, and in total control of their lives. If that's the case, does that mean that Cartcher and Litton

106

and the women I met at the gym are aberrations? Or because they're lesbians they're out of tune with other women? Help me out here, Bev."

Beverly finished chewing and wiped her mouth and hands and tossed the balled-up napkin in the trash. "I'm not sure what you want, Mimi. You know we live in a society that values youth and physical beauty, and you know that even young, beautiful women are still undervalued by this society. So, what's in store for a fifty-something woman? Sue's right, where's she going to find a lover, male or female? Fifty-something men marry thirty-something women. Women hurt themselves trying to conform to the cultural standard of beauty, whether it's by lifting too much weight in the gym or having the weight liposuctioned off or parts of the body lifted and tucked. You already know all this stuff, Mimi, so what is it you want from me?"

"I'm not sure," Mimi said, "though I thought I knew when I walked in the door. Maybe I just wanted to bring you Ethiopian food."

"Wanna know what I think?" Bev asked, and when Mimi nodded, she told her: "I think you wanted to hear that it's all right for you to write about human emotion instead of human weakness. Anybody—female or male—lucky enough to live long enough, will confront the consequences of aging, but not many people steal from their employers and go to jail. And those are the stories you know best."

Mimi stood up but there wasn't enough room to pace, so she sat back down. "Sue said that Kate was angry about being fifty and about the changes that came with growing older."

"Do you know that more women know more about breast cancer than they do about menopause?" Bev asked. "And while that's certainly important information to have, not every woman will get breast cancer. *Every* woman *will* go through menopause if she lives long enough, yet most women still have no idea what, exactly, that means."

"But is it really that big a deal if everybody does it? I

guess that's the question I need answered."

"Look at Kate and Sue and you tell me. Ask yourself how you'd feel if you lost all interest in sex and didn't know why or what to do about it."

"Sue said that didn't always happen."

"She's right," Bev said, "but it happens often enough and it's only one of perhaps a dozen symptoms--"

"A *dozen?*" Mimi yelped. "Sue mentioned three."

"You're familiar with the term peri-menopause?"

"Well, yeah, but--"

"But it doesn't apply to you? Don't end up like your friend, Kate, caught off guard and resentful and angry about the most natural occurrence of your life. In the next three to five years, Mimi, if not sooner, you'll begin to notice some subtle shifts and changes if you're paying attention to your body--"

Mimi jumped up and this time managed to find enough room to pace. "What do you mean in the next three to five years, Bev? I'm only forty!"

The amusement Bev had struggled to contain burst free and she started to giggle. "You should see yourself, Mimi, you look like...like...I don't know what!"

"This isn't funny! Why do I have to start worrying about this stuff now?"

"You don't have to *worry* about it at all, Mimi, and maybe that's where you should begin to think about your story: why do we worry about the most natural event in the universe?"

"So I should do a story that explains why we shouldn't have to worry about menopause?"

Bev looked at her watch, gave Mimi a tight hug and gentle kiss, and led her to the door. "It'll be enough if you do a story that just asks why it is we do worry."

The wind had shifted direction, Mimi noticed as soon as she stepped outside, and was blowing much colder. If it weren't so early in the season she'd believe that it held moisture, but she preferred to hold to the folklore that D.C. didn't get snow before

Thanksgiving. In fact, D.C. rarely got snow before Christmas, and almost never so early in November. And besides, the globe was supposed to be warming. She got into her car, turned the ignition on, and while she sat there waiting for the heater to come alive she paged through her notes, not really seeing what was written there. She was thinking about what Beverly had said, and how she was feeling about it— strangely off balance— and she wondered why. Sure, part of it was that business about peri-menopausal symptoms rearing their fuzzy little heads in the next couple or three years, and she'd have to deal with that. How? And when, exactly? When it happened, or before? And if she didn't deal with it early on, how would she know what was happening until it happened? Is this what Bev meant by asking the questions?

She looked down at her notebook again. *"The Wisdom of Menopause"* by a physician named Christiane Northrup is the book Bev suggested she read.

"Shit," she muttered, shifting the car into gear and screeching out of the parking space, "like I already don't have enough to worry about without adding menopause to the list." *You don't have to worry at all,* she heard Bev say, and she realized that she was Everywoman. Enlightened and knowledgeable about all manner of 21st century techno crap and woefully ignorant about a million-year old phenomenon that was the most natural occurrence in the universe.

It was a short drive from Bev's Midtown Psychotherapy Associates in the Shaw neighborhood, north on 13th Street and then west on U Street to SisterSpace Books. They'd have the Northrup book and other helpful titles as well. But so what? Helpful as the information might be, it wasn't a story. Was it? Could she make her editor and his editor and his editor— three forty-something men— care why women worried themselves sick over what was natural and normal? Would they care if they thought their wives would be affected? Suppose their wives didn't get face and breast lifts and liposuctions; suppose they didn't dye their hair; suppose they lost interest in sex and didn't know why or what to do about it? Would these men she knew abandon those wives in favor of younger women? And would these women then be susceptible to behavior that could get them killed? Mimi pulled over to the curb, out of traffic, and shut off the engine. Too many thoughts and ideas were competing for attention, interfering with the one thing she wanted to think of, which was to remember the name of Marianne and Renee's other bar and where exactly it was. Somewhere between D.C. and Baltimore. Frederick? Columbia! And they'd sold the place, they hadn't closed it. It was still there, the place where, according to Sue and Kate's friend, Sarah, Ellie Litton had met her new lover for drinks. Ellie Litton, who'd moved to Columbia to be near her new lover. *Happy Landings* it was called and it was on the bank of a small lake that froze solid in the winter. Sarah said Ellie had taken the name to be an omen. Had the veterinarian from Georgia, Millicent Cartcher, thought the same thing, that she'd finally made a happy landing? Before both women crash landed.

CHAPTER EIGHT

"No computer is ever totally clean, Boss," Kenny Chang was saying as his fingers danced across the keyboard of Sandra Phillips's computer while Linda Lopez and Cassie Ali, seated on either side of him, talked him through an array of unlocking and data restoration programs, most of them known to and available only to law enforcement agencies. Sandy's computer and a thick sheaf of downloaded, printed e-mails found taped inside a statistical research notebook were with the Hate Crimes team in the Think Tank. All of Sandy Phillips's other possessions were being loaded on to Raul Lozano's truck— by Lozano and three new graduates of the police academy— for transport and delivery to an address in Galveston, Texas, an address that was a three-story, climate controlled storage facility. So far, all they'd been able to learn was that the same company that had hired Lozano had rented the storage facility in Galveston, but neither the company nor the person who signed Lozano's contract existed in Galveston or in Poolesville, Maryland, where Lozano's company was based. Arrangements were made with police in Galveston to detain whoever showed up to claim Sandra Phillips's belongings, and Gianna and her team turned their focus to that which they could do something about.

There were two hundred and sixty-two email messages between Sandy Phillips and somebody named Spice, email address "NICENSPICE." More than half of them were copies of the messages Sandy had sent to Spice, printed out after she'd sent them and saved neatly and meticulously by date. The others were from Spice to Sandy and downloaded after she'd received them, in direct violation of Spice's order to delete them immediately. *"Until I'm free to be with you, to be fully and truly yours, I must conceal my love...my lust for you. Do not save these messages. Delete them immediately, and carry my love in your heart."* Seven times, over five months, Spice had directed Sandy Phillips to delete the messages.

Sandy had disobeyed, and for that Gianna was grateful, though she wasn't certain that Sandy's disobedience ultimately would benefit their investigation. Every one of Spice's messages had been sent from a public location— a library or a cyber cafe or an airport or a hotel— with no way to trace the transmission back to her.

"Somebody who knew what they were doing has been in this computer, Boss," Kenny said, not looking up from the screen, his fingers not ceasing their tap-tap- tapping. "They left evidence that they've been in here, but they did a good job of deleting anything that could help us and a good job covering their tracks. Good thing we found those emails."

Gianna didn't bother to point out that the emails hadn't helped bring them a single step closer to identifying the killer; that in fact the emails would be of no use unless and until they identified the killer by other means, and could tie her— or him— to the victim. Kenny knew this, as did they all. But it felt better to cling to any little bit of evidence in a case like this, no matter now flimsy, than to admit the truth. And the truth was, unless the killer of Sandra Phillips and the other women made a big mistake, she most likely would go unpunished. And it *was* a she, Gianna thought. The more she studied the victims and the circumstances of their lives and the paths that led to their deaths, the more convinced she was that a woman was responsible.

Three investigators from the Missing Persons Bureau were in the field, feeding back information daily on the past lives of Ellie Litton, Millicent Cartcher, Sandy Phillips and Mabel Gunther. Gianna couldn't wait for the investigators to return to D.C. and file their written reports; she had to talk to them every day, to latch on to any and every detail and piece of information that helped fill in the blank spaces of the women's lives. And while the information she was amassing wouldn't amount to much in terms of evidence in a trial, it spoke volumes about the women and how they came to be victims. That information, in aggregate, was what helped Gianna conclude that the killer was a woman. Now, if only she'd make a mistake.

"If you're not getting anything useful, Kenny, give it up. Don't waste any more time looking for something that's not there. You and Cassie and Linda get back to the victim files. We'll have photographs of each victim by late tomorrow."

"Then can I get back outside, Boss?"

"You can continue to do what you're doing, which is to make certain you know everything there is to know about Ellie Litton and how she lived her life. And when her photo comes, certainly you can canvass her neighborhood and job site. Ditto for you, Kenny and Linda, with the photos of Millie Cartcher and Mable Gunther. Maybe there's a piece of luck for us out there."

Had she been in a better mood Gianna would have added that she hoped and prayed for a piece of luck; such an admission of humanity would have taken the sting out of her reproach of Cassie. But she wasn't feeling especially benevolent, and she wasn't feeling like admitting out loud that luck was what they'd need to find Spice.

Gianna stood, stretched her back, and walked over to the blackboard where they hung all of the crime scene photos and the cause of death page from each of the post mortem exams. She knew exactly what she'd see, but she looked again anyway. No doubt the murders had been committed by the same person, but when she looked closely at the photos she had doubts. All the psychological evidence pointed to a female perp; but when it came to the physical evidence— the piano wire slicing through the esophagi of the victims— she had to admit that she had trouble envisioning a woman performing such an act more than once. Certainly there were women physically capable. She probably was physically capable herself. And certainly there were evil women— enough that major metropolises didn't have enough cells in the women's wings of their jails to house them all. But Gianna couldn't help thinking that something else fueled these crimes, and though she wasn't sure exactly what it was, it wasn't something that was common to women. A broken heart might kill once, but not six times.

113

"Money," she said. "Talk to the personnel people at Ellie Litton's job again and find out if she had direct deposit to a bank. Find out what happened to Millie Cartcher's Reston condo. Talk to the field reps and have them check on hometown bank accounts. And Linda, the banks here, the big ones, see if there are or were accounts in any of the vics' names." All that new stuff, Gianna thought, and the homes completely cleaned out. New clothes, new furniture. Greed, not hatred, perhaps; just plain old garden variety greed.

She withdrew from her reverie and turned around when the door flew open and crashed against the wall. Eric Ashby rushed in, Bobby Gilliam, Tim McCreedy and Tony Watkins hard on his heels. "You've got 'em."

"Good as got 'em," Eric said nodding. "The truck's northbound on I-85 in North Carolina. If they don't stop, they'll be in Virginia before sundown, and given the forecast, I'd guess they'll keep on driving, keep trying to eat up as much highway as possible."

"What forecast?"

"Rain, freezing rain, sleet."

"Oh bloody hell!" Gianna looked at her watch, then at Cassie, Kenny and Linda, who were watching her carefully and expectantly. "In case you hadn't guessed, our Irish gun runners are in the cross-hairs. I'm going to be out of pocket I hope for no longer than it takes to drive down to the North Carolina line and back. Alice is on the bar angle. I want you three to keep doing what you're doing— and keep Alice in the loop. I don't want this office left unattended for a single moment. You all can decide among yourselves how to handle that." She looked at her watch again. "Freezing rain and sleet," she muttered. "Let me get my boots out of my office and I'm ready."

Mimi scowled at the enormous television set mounted on the wall above the mirror at the far end of the *Happy Landings* bar. She didn't know whether she was more irritated at what she'd seen on the screen in the last half hour or by the fact that she actually was spending her time staring at the thing, trying to make sense of the dialogue and the action. The movie was as stupid as anything she'd ever seen and she'd seen a lot of television in recent days, following Bev's suggestion that she give herself a dose of popular culture. Erin, the bartender, had proclaimed herself a fan of the movie's star, a stranger to Mimi and who couldn't act to save her life. Which could account for the fact that she was about to be raped for the second time. Why would anybody want to watch this crap? Why would anybody spend the money to make it? And this was supposed to be television for women. "Wonder what television for men would be like?" she muttered, using all her will power to resist the urge to get up and leave. She obviously hadn't missed much by tuning out popular culture. But then there *were* those commercials for products to relieve the symptoms of menopause. She especially liked the one with Lauren Hutton, who didn't look as if she'd gained a single pound or lost a single hair.

She gave up on the movie and turned her attention to her surroundings. She hadn't been to this bar in at least four years, but clearly things had changed. It was not a large place and it was longer than it was wide, but Mimi thought that it was not quite so dark and gloomy as before. Her glance circled the room again. There now were mirrors and track lighting and a living room-like grouping of furniture at the far, narrow end of the room opposite the bar in front of a gas fireplace which burned as cheerily as if it were the real thing. The place was cozy now; so much so that Mimi almost picked up her drink and moved to the fireplace. She had to remind herself that just because it was raw and cold and windy outside didn't mean that she was free to seek the comfort of a fire. She was here to work; to chat up the bartender; to learn whether there existed a connection between Ellie Litton's presence here and her murder. Which meant striking up a conversation with Erin who, upon closer inspection, bore a strong resemblance to the actress, Michelle Pfeiffer.

115

Erin had washed glasses and dumped cherries from a huge plastic tub into a smaller container and now was cutting lemons and limes, and ignoring the gigantic tin of peanuts that Mimi was waiting for her to open. One eye on the television screen, the other on the lemons and limes — not much chance that she'd see Mimi pretending to be dying for another vodka and tonic and a bowl of peanuts. Maybe if she went to the bathroom and came back, Erin would notice her. Maybe if she spilled her drink...no, not a good idea, since what was in her glass was water and not the vodka and tonic Erin had poured half an hour ago. That concoction was down the toilet, replaced by water from the bottle in Mimi's purse. She slurped up the remainder, tilted her head and glass back to get the ice bits, and lightly plopped the empty glass down on the bar. Erin heard, good barkeep that she was.

"Be right with you," she called out.

"Bring some nuts with you?" Mimi queried.

In answer, Erin grabbed bowls from a shelf beneath the bar and deftly poured nuts from the can into the bowls. Then she mixed Mimi's drink and brought glass and bowl to her.

"You've got this bartending business down to a science," Mimi said with real appreciation as she placed a bill on the counter and waved away Erin's move to make change from the pockets of her apron. "You must have been at it for a while."

"Thanks," Erin said with the kind of head movement that signaled her appreciation for both the tip and the acknowledgement of her professionalism. She was a fairly tall woman— taller than Mimi— with a head full of the kind of thick, red-brown hair that less blessed women pay good money for— and which was prettier by far than Michelle's limp blonde locks. When she smiled, her eyes literally sparkled, and the laugh lines around them suggested that was a regular habit.

"I hope it's not rude to say so, but you don't look old enough to have been legal in bars long enough to pick up those skills." That earned Mimi a full grin from Erin, whose baby blues twinkled.

116

"My Dad and my uncles owned a bar in Reisterstown, back when it was a working mill town, and since I couldn't go to work at the mills I went to work in the bar when I was fifteen and I've been at it ever since. It's my kinda work."

"You knew when you were that young?"

Erin nodded and smiled the smile that lit her face. "And I knew I wanted my own place one day. When this came up for sale, me and Jackie snatched it up before Marianne and Renee could even hang the For Sale sign in the window."

"Is Jackie your lover?"

Erin's good mood evaporated. "Why do you ask?" The question was a challenge and Mimi knew she had to rise to the occasion without knowing why.

"It takes a lot of work to create a good place, and this is a good place. It looks good, it feels good. You both should be proud," Mimi said.

"We are," Erin said, "though I don't have a clue why you'd care. What are you doing out in this neck of the woods anyway?" She shifted gears so smoothly that Mimi missed a beat and actually had to take a sip of the vodka and tonic to recover her wits.

"Going through some changes." The lie rolled out smoothly. "I used to come out here years ago, though not in the winter," she said with a grimace. "It's a good place to come to get out of the city."

Erin rolled her eyes. "You married or is your lover married?" And at the look on Mimi's face, her expression changed. "You all think nobody knows what you're up to? Being gay's not a game you play when you're bored with your life, you know. Have a fling with a woman and then run back to some man."

"I....I...I'm not playing any kind of game," Mimi sputtered. She was so completely surprised by Erin's assessment of the reason for her presence that she couldn't talk. Sure, she was here under false pretenses, but not *those* false pretenses. "I just wanted to get away from the city, like I said. I was at the opening of Marianne and Renee's new place, and that made me think of this place, and I just thought I'd see what was happening out here. Just a change of pace, you know?"

"Sure," Erin said, pulling a towel from her waist band and wiping down the bar in front of Mimi where her glass had left a wet spot. "And I suppose you got some swampland in Arizona you'd like me to take a look at."

"Sounds like you don't like outsiders. Is this one of those places in books and movies where the residents are gentle and peace-loving until a stranger shows up? Then the stranger's body parts begin emerging from the landfill--"

"You think that's funny?" Erin's snarl was frightening. Her face no longer looked young and innocent and pretty. "You don't have the right to laugh at who and what I am just because you're from D.C."

"How do you know I'm from D.C.? I could be from Baltimore."

"How many times, in how many different ways, are you gonna call me stupid?"

Mimi inhaled and waited, but no words would come that could adequately respond to Erin's accusation. As an observer and a chronicler of events and circumstances, she would certainly claim to be able to tell the difference between someone from Baltimore and D.C. by looking at her. Why wouldn't she endow Erin with that ability? Especially Erin, a bartender, who was probably better at judging character than she was? "It wasn't my intention to insult you, Erin, and I'm sorry if I did. I was just making small talk, trying for humor, and it seems like I picked a tender topic."

"Damn right it's tender, Miss D.C.! Something happens to somebody and right away we're like the people from that hillbilly movie— we must have done something to 'em! But you're right about one thing, and that's how people who are different do stand out. I welcome anybody in my bar, but it *is* a lesbian bar. That's who comes in here and that's who I *want* to

118

come in here."

Damn! Erin herself just opened the door to discussion of Ellie Litton and Mimi couldn't take advantage because the other woman was angry with her. And justifiably so; she'd said some stupid things. Mimi released the breath she'd been holding. "You're a tough one, Erin. What do I have to do to convince you that I'm not straight, that I'm not here to meet a straight woman that, at the very worst I'm playing hooky from my job, that I just felt like getting out of the city for a few hours?"

She raised her palms in an I-surrender gesture. Erin looked directly at her, holding her gaze, then looked past her. Her eyes changed from sparkling blue to storm-cloud gray.

"Tell me you don't know her," she said. "Tell me she's not here for you."

Mimi turned around as the door opened, admitting, on a gust of raw, wet wind, as stunning a woman as she'd ever seen. "I don't know her," she said to Erin, "but I could do something about that if it would make you feel better."

Erin gave Mimi a dry, wry laugh, told her she was full of shit, and strolled off to the other end of the bar to resume her preparations for the Happy Hour crowd, and to check on the progress of her movie heroine. Mimi, annoyed at having lost the chance to probe Erin about Ellie and maybe Millicent Cartcher, took too big a sip of her drink, forgetting it was real alcohol, and choked.

"Want me to slap you on the back?" The voice was low, slow, and pure southern. It held a hint of humor and quite a lot of real good will, and when Mimi continued to cough without answering, the woman clapped her on the back a couple of times. "Strong spirits can do that to you if you're not careful."

Mimi swiveled around on the bar stool. "Thanks for the advice." She extended her hand and introduced herself. Alice Long returned the gesture in kind.

"Did you just get here?" Mimi asked, realizing as soon as the words were out of her mouth how rude the question was, and

119

grateful that Alice found humor in the rudeness.

"You think my accent's thick, you oughta hear my sister, and she's been in New York longer than I've been here. I guess we're like Arnold Schwartzenegger and Henry Kissinger. No matter how long we're in a place, we'll always sound like we just got off the boat. But it hasn't seemed to hurt them any, has it?"

"*Touché,*" Mimi said. "May I buy you a drink to apologize?"

"Sure, as long as it's not what you're drinking," Alice said with a grimace. "I'll let you off cheap. I'll have a club soda with a twist of lime. And another bowl of those peanuts. I missed lunch today and I'm starving."

Mimi signaled Erin, who gave her a sideways look when she approached, and took the order without comment. But Alice commented and Mimi felt she had to explain what had transpired between herself and the bartender immediately prior to Alice's arrival. "So she thinks you're straight? Or that I am? And is she saying that this is some kind of rendezvous spot for local Ann Heches and Julie Cyphers?"

Alice's response put Mimi instantly on alert but she tried to cover her reaction. She shrugged and grabbed a handful of peanuts which she put into her mouth, one at a time, and slowly chewed, while she watched Alice take a long drink of her club soda. She watched Alice close up at the realization that she was being watched, leaving Mimi nothing to observe but what was there on the surface. Which, without a doubt, was well worth observing. Alice was dark brown with startling light brown eyes that held a steady but not threatening gaze, and Mimi guessed that they were about the same height. Alice wore heavy black tights that revealed the muscles in her legs, a black turtle neck sweater, and a leather aviator jacket, an old one with a fur collar. Doc Martens on her feet and a black watch cap on her head. Alice Long definitely wasn't a local. And the way she relaxed her body but kept her eyes on alert was all too familiar to Mimi.

"Are you a regular here?"

120

Alice held Mimi in her steady gaze, growing surprised when Mimi didn't blink. "My first time here, as a matter of fact," Alice replied, lobbing back a question of her own: "How about you? You a regular here?"

"I'm not a regular anywhere. I drop in now and again when and where it suits me." Mimi slid forward on the barstool and planted her feet flat on the floor and leaned in toward Alice, encroaching on her space. Alice didn't flinch.

"And it suited you today to be all the way out here? Why is that?"

"Probably for many of the same reasons you fled D.C. today," Mimi replied. "Unless, of course, you really are a straight woman in hiding or denial."

"In which case you'd be pleased to save me from myself?"

Alice was only half kidding and Mimi knew she was out of her element. Actually, she was rusty from a few years of good behavior. Marianne's comment the other night about her past behavior had been right on the mark and it was the break-up with Beverly that had caused Mimi to take a close look at herself. Bev, who had urged her to "stay away from women if you can't treat us any better than men treat us." And she had stayed away until she met Gianna. And her behavior had been impeccable. Until she met Alice Long, and though she hadn't misbehaved, she certainly was considering it; had been from the moment the wind blew Alice into *Happy Landings*. Then she remembered that Alice Long most likely was a cop and her ardor cooled. One cop per lifetime was sufficient. She looked at her watch.

"Well, damn," Alice drawled. "That's as major a dismissal as I've ever gotten. I'm guessing it was something I said," she said.

Mimi shook her head. "You can't seriously believe that anybody could dismiss you, Alice, for any reason. You mentioned being hungry. I'm hungry, too, and I was checking to see if it made more sense to eat here or go back to D.C."

"You keep saying I'm from D.C. I never said I was from

121

D.C."

"They used to make a pretty good shrimp salad plate here," Mimi said, ignoring the bit about D.C., and before Alice could reply, the door blew open, letting in a stronger, colder, wetter gust of arctic air. Four women rode in on it, laughing and talking and stamping their feet and blowing on their hands. Erin began fixing their drinks before the door closed. Happy Hour had begun at *Happy Landings*. This is what Mimi had come here for. Alice, too, judging by the way she studied the women. They all appeared to be fifty-something and as they shed coats and scarves, their wardrobe suggested that they might be mid-level office workers: well-made pant suits all around, good but not flashy jewelry, short, well-maintained, beauty parlor haircuts, no make up to speak of. Three were white, one was black, and they were relaxed and chatty, sailing into the bar like a ship too long at sea. By the time they'd hung their coats on a wall rack and seated themselves around the table nearest Erin's end of the bar, she had their drinks on a tray along with two bowls of nuts, and was headed their way. The exchange among the women was light and easy, with lots of laughter, some of it raucous when accompanied by sly glances at the newcomers at the bar. Erin propped her elbows on the table and leaned across it; the four women leaned in close to her, and after a few seconds of concentrated silence, the room exploded with laugher.

"Think we're topic A?" Mimi asked.

"Don't be such a swell head," Alice drawled, and Mimi chuckled. She had to keep reminding herself that not only was this woman probably a cop, but given her presence at this bar and her obvious interest in the clientele, she could well be connected to Gianna and the Hate Crimes Unit. Without that in the way, however, Mimi could, she thought, find herself fully enjoying the company of Alice Long.

"How're your drinks?" Erin said from behind them, and they swiveled around to face her.

"Do you still have that shrimp salad plate?"

Erin shook her head. "But we've got crab cakes tonight. My mama makes 'em. But it's just crab cakes and fries because we don't have a full kitchen."

"If your mama makes good crab cakes, you don't need a full kitchen," Alice said. Then she squinted at Erin. "Can your mama make good crab cakes?"

"The best this far west of the Eastern Shore," Erin declared.

By the time they were able to testify to the veracity of Erin's claim about her mother's ability with crab cakes, Happy Hour was in full swing and the crowd made the bar seem even smaller than it was. Mimi and Alice had moved to a table which they now shared with three other women who also devoured the crab cakes and fries and were willing to marry Erin's mother sight unseen. The other four tables were full, as were the sofa and chairs around the fireplace. It was standing room only at the bar, which is also where the most noise was. Mimi realized that there was no music in this bar. Just the television, which at the moment, was tuned— loudly— to a basketball game. She didn't know who was playing, only that there definitely was partisanship among the viewers. A loud cheer rose then abated as a commercial appeared on the screen. Mimi was about to tune back in to the conversation at her table when there was a definite energy shift at the bar. The raised voices were ugly and angry.

"I said turn the goddamn thing off! I'm fuckin' sick and tired of jiggling tits in beer commercials!" one voice roared above the others. "These stupid-ass beer ads are gonna make me stop drinking beer, I swear to God!"

There apparently was significant support for that point of view because a cheer was raised in the room from as far away as the fireplace. The television station was changed. Somebody requested Xena and in a few seconds, the Warrior Princess, yips, yodels, grimaces and all, filled the screen and the warm fuzzies returned to the atmosphere in the bar.

Mimi turned back toward the table in time to see Alice

sink back into her chair and remove her hand from beneath her jacket. She doubted that anyone else had noticed but Alice saw that she had, and her eyes narrowed. "A friend of mine said the same thing just the other day about beer commercials," Mimi said into the relative silence that now permeated the room.

"I already quit drinking the stuff," one of the women at the table said. "It's insulting the way they use women. Like they can't sell beer without tits."

"And do you think those young women who make those commercials give any kind of thought to what it is they're doing?" asked another woman, to simultaneous snorts of "hell, no!" from her friends.

"Somebody better tell 'em that they're gonna wake up one day and firm tits and a tight ass will be things of the past."

"Those young girls don't want to hear that stuff, and wouldn't believe you if you told 'em. You didn't when you were that age."

Mimi and Alice both were so tuned in to the talk swirling around them they weren't aware that the latest gust of wind had delivered a member of the Maryland State Patrol, who had walked purposefully to the bar. Erin immediately muted the sound on Xena, which is what got the room's attention.

"I'm not driving, Helen, I swear I'm not!" somebody called out from the back of the room, and the crowd, including Trooper Helen, cracked up.

"You lie, Wanda," Helen called out good naturedly, "and I'm gonna catch you one of these nights. And when I do!" Helen had to raise her hands to quiet the loud guffaws that spread through the room. "Hate to do this to you, Erin, but anybody who's driving better hit the road now. The forecasters got one right for a change: The sleet and freezing rain is moving in fast. The secondary roads are already slick."

Helen's voice was over-ridden by the sound of chairs scraping the floor as every woman in the place stood up. Mimi had already paid for her dinner and Alice's, so she grabbed her coat and headed for the door, Alice on her heels, after they had exchanged hugs with the women at their table and the hope that they'd see each other again.

"I hate ice!" Mimi exclaimed as the prickly moisture stung her face. '

"Me too," Alice agreed, pulling her cap down lower over her ears. They faced each other in the parking lot, women rushing to their cars, engines starting, headlights creating the illusion of warmth. "Think we can get together again?"

Mimi hesitated, unsure of herself for the first time in a long time. "How about at *The Bayou,* one evening next week?"

"Which evening?"

"How's Wednesday," Mimi said, "seven-thirty?" and, receiving an over-the- shoulder wave from Alice, she hurried to her car, praying that she'd make it home before the roads iced and became treacherous.

Eric Ashby whipped the steering wheel from side to side, cursing under his breath and, finally, risking a light tap of the brake. The SUV regained traction and Eric and Gianna regained their heartbeats. "If I wreck my truck out here looking for some damn Irish gun runners, I'm going to seek retribution."

"Would you settle for reimbursement?" Gianna asked.

"Hell no! I'd want to kick some Irish ass."

"Isn't there something not quite right about cops seeking retribution?"

"Only if it becomes public knowledge," Eric replied, and Gianna made a zipping motion with her fingers across her lips. "I feel so much safer," Eric said.

"That makes one of us," Gianna said. "I'm terrified. I hate ice." She peered ahead into the darkness. Nothing but blinking red taillights as far as she could see. They were just south of Richmond, on I-95 and traffic would be dense this time of evening anyway. But with the roads icing and the Department of Sanitation trucks spreading salt and sand, traffic was at a virtual standstill. "But if we can't move any faster, they can't, either."

"I just hope there isn't an accident or something that pulls our guy off before we can establish surveillance."

"I'll second that," Gianna said, and looked at her watch. It had been exactly thirty-two minutes since their last contact with the Virginia State Trooper who had first sighted the blue van with the mismatched D.C. license plates on northbound Interstate 85 in Southern Virginia, acknowledged the APB, and then followed it toward Washington. Their plan was that the D.C. officers would intercept the van just south of Richmond, where I-85 and I-95 merge, and, assuming that the van would travel 95 north into D.C., take over surveillance and stop the truck as soon as it crossed the line into D.C., the illegal tags being sufficient reason for a stop. In a way, the weather was working in their favor, since the presence of cops on the highway in a weather emergency would be expected and would give the guys in the van no reason to worry. But given the Florida mechanic's assessment of the condition of the van, Gianna could only pray that it would survive another couple of hours on icy roads. She checked her watch again. "Our exit's coming up."

Eric had already seen the sign announcing it. He picked up his cell phone, hit a button, and waited. "Can you get permission for us to ride the shoulder for one eighth of a mile....that's all it is, I swear! I can see the sign. But traffic is at a dead halt going south and it's moving northbound. The bastards'll pass us while we sit here...of course she's here!" He rolled his eyes and gave her the phone.

"Who is this?" she snapped, only half her irritation feigned. "Of course I'm right here, where else would I be?" She held the phone away from her face and gave it an evil look before replacing it to her ear. "Yes, Sergeant, the request applies to Officers Gilliam, McCreedy and Watkins as well. They're right behind us. We appreciate your help. You probably insured the success of our mission this evening." She punched off the phone, tossed it back to Eric, rolled down the window and put the light

126

on top. The truck shimmied a bit as it left the highway but Eric quickly regained control, hit the switch that activated the light, and reached the exit in a less than a minute, the sedan carrying Bobby Gilliam, Tim McCreedy and Tony Watkins riding their bumper.

It took almost half an hour to reach the road from the exit ramp and cross over the freeway and re-enter it heading north, but just as they did, the radio crackled. At the same moment, they saw the Virginia State Trooper car that they'd been in communication with for most of the day. And Gianna saw the blue van carrying the four Irish nationals and they didn't know how many weapons. She picked up the radio and thanked the trooper with the promise that if he ever needed any help from D.C., he was to call her directly. She promised again— she'd made the same promise at least half a dozen times that day— that she and her people would take no aggressive action while in Virginia, and it was a promise that she'd keep. The Virginia Trooper was needed back at his barracks and the worsening weather situation meant that there would be no extra bodies to assign to help out a neighboring jurisdiction.

"I just hope that rattle trap of theirs will make it back to D.C. tonight," Gianna said. "I really don't want to spend the night in this truck."

"What's wrong with my truck?"

"It's a lovely truck, Eric, but it doesn't have mattresses and pillows and heat when the engine's turned off. In short, the comforts of home are sorely lacking."

"Speaking of which, I hope you thanked Miss Patterson properly. Without her assistance we wouldn't have known where the guns were until the Ganjas were fighting the Irishmen for them."

"Oh, spare me the Be Kind to Miss Patterson lecture."

"Come on, Anna, she deserves it."

"The last thing I need is to have her thinking I'm indebted to her. She's already impossible to get along with."

Eric and Gianna had known each other since their police academy days, and they'd become close friends when he challenged a class macho man who wouldn't accept Gianna's "no" for what it meant. Eric had spent his high school days defending a gay younger brother from bullies; defending a friend and classmate came easily. Less easy to accept sometimes was her prickly nature, exacerbated by the pressures of being a lieutenant, of heading a unit, of being a woman, of being a lesbian. To show her that he'd never cross the line between them, he still called her Anna, the derivative of Giovanna, which was her name. Gianna was the family name, the pet name, the name reserved for only those closest to her. He could claim that privilege; he chose not to, out of respect.

They let the conversation lapse as they both kept their eyes glued to the blue van directly ahead of them. It truly was as raggedy as anything on the road, but it was rolling along at a decent clip. Eric jerked his head to the left and Gianna saw the sedan carrying Bobby, Tim and Tony pull alongside them. She watched it as it moved up beside the blue van. She saw it pull ahead, then saw the right turn signal flash, and it was in front of the van. They had 'em boxed in. By-the-book perfect.

"Why did we have to do this?" Eric asked, as he, too, felt the relief of knowing that they'd almost completed their mission and had done it by the book.

"Because we were ordered to do it."

"Gimme a break, would ya?" He didn't try to conceal the disgust in his voice. He was irritated that she'd feed him the same line she'd fed the Unit. She reached across the truck's cab and grabbed his shoulder and squeezed.

"That's all the truth I know, Eric. He called me into his office and told me to do it. At the same time he told me to activate Cassie or release her."

"So she was right. We're going to be budget chopped."

Gianna didn't answer and neither of them spoke again for another three hours, until they were in the tunnel beneath New

York Avenue. The streets in D.C. were practically deserted, which was good. But since the blue van hadn't stopped, it was a good guess that they had some means of mobile communication with whoever was waiting for them, and the Shamrock Bar was nearby. However, as they emerged from the tunnel's mouth, they were quickly surrounded by D.C. cop cars. Gianna watched as Tony Watkins sped ahead of the blue van then whipped the sedan sideways so that it blocked the street. Eric sped up so that he was on the van's bumper, but the van didn't stop moving until it reached the sedan carrying Bobby and Tony that was blocking the road. They were out of the vehicle, weapons drawn and aimed at the blue van. The other cops now were out and the blue van was surrounded. Gianna and Eric got out of the truck.

The street was treacherously slick and Gianna lost her footing and slid into the truck. She waved Eric ahead, toward the action, and took a minute to regain her balance, and watched as both passenger doors of the blue van opened and the driver and front seat passenger emerged. They looked exactly as Mimi had described them and Gianna did indeed owe her. Responding to commands shouted through a bullhorn, the two men lay face down in the street, their hands behind their heads, their legs crossed at the ankles. Gianna hoped for their sakes that it was a smooth take-down because it was too cold to lay too long on the icy street. And it was still raining ice pellets, cold, hard, prickly rocks that stung the skin.

The blue van now was surrounded by cops keeping their distance, since it was known that the van contained weapons. They ordered the remaining inhabitants to open the van's rear doors, show their hands, and emerge, one at a time. After a brief wait, the panel door slid open and three other men stepped out. Gianna was surprised; she expected a total of four. That's how many Mimi had seen, that's how many the café manager in Florida had seen, that's how many the Florida mechanic had seen. Had there been a fifth man all along or had he joined the group somewhere along the drive north?

The first two out of the van were handcuffed and inside the SWAT trucks. The remaining three, now spread-eagle on the frigid street, soon would be cuffed and safely locked inside the truck, and Gianna could call the Chief and tell him he could relax. Then she could....something moved off to her right, something just out of her sightline. She backed up until she was touching Eric's truck and scanned the area directly in front of her. SWAT now had control of the blue van. All the doors were open and the crime scene technicians were about to begin their work. All five suspects were cuffed and in custody. Now she heard something. She cocked her head and listened. Ice falling from the sky and hitting the ground and sounding like ball bearings dropped on a hardwood floor, car tires in the distance, swishing in the accumulating slush. And something else. She passed her eyes back and forth across the scene like a searchlight.

"*Hey!*" It was a surprised, angry yell from a cop looking her way, looking past her. She turned to see a figure running— slipping and sliding— back into the tunnel. She whipped around and gave chase. She and the perp lost their traction and fell at the same time. She scrambled to her knees, crawled a few feet, slid a few more, stood, ran for several yards, and when she fell again, she was almost upon the perp who apparently had injured himself when he fell.

"Police! Stop!" she yelled, and he rolled over, saw her, and struggled to his feet. He was limping badly. When he fell again, Gianna was on top of him. Maybe he'd hurt a leg or a knee, but there was nothing wrong with his fists. He punched at her, landing several solid blows to her chest and midsection, and he delivered a head butt that had she taken it on her forehead would have knocked her unconscious. But it landed on the side of her face, down near her neck, and was painful enough that she released the hold she had on his arm and he scrambled away from her. She reached out and grabbed a leg just before he crawled out of reach, and it must have been the injured leg because he howled in pain. Gianna straddled him, pinning his arms to the ground

130

and avoiding proximity to his head. She was immediately relieved by a phalanx of slipping, sliding cops led by Tim McCreedy, who pulled her upright and into a steadying grip.

"How the hell did he get free?" Gianna demanded of nobody in particular, freeing herself from Tim's grasp.

"Fuckin' hole in the bottom of the van," an out-of-breath Eric Ashby said, sliding to a stop beside her. "Are you all right?"

'I'm fine," she said, including both Eric and Tim. "Why was there a hole in the floor of the truck?"

"To load and unload their weapons without being seen." This from a SWAT lieutenant that she knew to be, like herself, a protégé of the chief, and whose badge identified him as **R. Gomez**.

"Jesus," Gianna muttered. "He could have taken out half of us before we knew what hit us."

"I could have lived the rest of my life without hearing that," Gomez said.

Gianna shrugged him an apology. She could have lived the rest of her life without having to think it. "You guys got this wrapped up, you think?"

Gomez nodded. "We're ready to run the perps in and the truck is here to tow the van to the lab. We'll have the street cleared in another fifteen or twenty."

Gianna nodded her thanks and was about to walk away to call the chief when Gomez touched her shoulder, drawing her back toward him. He leaned in close.

"I'm glad to meet you. I've heard a lot about you, apparently a lot of it lies. You did good out here tonight. I don't know how you caught him on this ice, but you've got a whole chorus of 'atta girls' coming your way." Then he clapped her on the shoulder and turned away, working, like everybody else, to keep his footing on the ice.

"What was that all about?" Eric asked.

"I don't know." But I don't like it, she thought. I don't like it worth a damn.

CHAPTER NINE

As soundly as Mimi could sleep through the ringing of the telephone in the middle of the night, she could awaken immediately and fully at the slightest sound or movement in her house. She had put the telephone on the pillow next to her head and set the ringer on loud in case Gianna called, and she'd fallen asleep at eleven-thirty with the brittle sound of sleet hitting the windows and the street. At four-twelve, according to the red digital readout on the clock face, she sat straight up in bed and listened: The garage door rising. She jumped up, grabbed her robe, and hurried down the hallway, through the living room and dining room and kitchen, and flung open the door as Gianna stepped gingerly from her sedan. The sleepy but welcome smile on Mimi's face froze.

"Good God, Gianna, what happened to you?" She rushed to her and could tell that her embrace was painful so she relaxed her hold, allowing Gianna to lean on her.

"You should see the other guy."

Mimi wasn't inclined toward humor. "I thought you promised the chief you were staying out of the fray."

Gianna groaned. "I've already listened to him give me grief, so don't you start, too. But for the record, the last thing I wanted was to chase some perp. You know how I hate ice."

"Obviously you caught him. Who was it?"

"One of your Irishmen."

"One of *my*..." Mimi sighed, wrapped her arms around Gianna. It was cold in the garage. "Come on, let's get you cleaned up and into bed. Are you hungry?"

"Ravenous. But you know what I'd really like?"

"What would you really like, Gianna me darlin'?" Mimi said with a passable imitation of a brogue.

"An hour in the hot tub and a drink."

132

Fifteen minutes later Gianna was up to her neck in hot, churning water, head thrown back, watching the rain-sleet-snow mixture hurl itself earthward from the black sky, compliments of the sky dome that covered what formerly was the tool shed attached to Mimi's garage. It wasn't a very large space but it was well-used. The floor was laid with Italian tile, the hot tub itself encased in brick and adobe, so that it resembled a fountain in the middle of a piazza. Ferns and spider plants thrived in the moist, steamy heat. It was a little corner of paradise, a perfect end to an imperfect day. Gianna had almost drifted off to sleep when Mimi returned with a wicker tray which she placed on the wide edge of the hot tub. Gianna opened her eyes to find a platter of feta cheese, black olives, sun dried tomatoes, a loaf of her favorite rosemary bread and a tumbler of chilled vodka. She reached for the vodka and took a long, slow sip.

"Oh, Lord, that's good!" She took another sip and put the glass back on the tray as Mimi stepped into the water. "But this is even better," she said, drawing Mimi down into her arms and into a kiss that increased the water temperature by several degrees. While she explored her mouth with her tongue, she explored her body with her hands. When finally she took her mouth from Mimi's mouth, she bit and nibbled her neck and her shoulder blade, which caused Mimi to squirm. And as she bent her head in search of a breast, Mimi stopped.

"I keep telling you that you're going to drown yourself in here one of these days. You're not an amphibian, my dear."

"Then come here," Gianna ordered, pulling Mimi into her lap to straddle her, and delivering delicious, erect nipples right to her mouth. She wrapped one arm around Mimi's back, pulling her in close; the other hand was wedged between them, between Mimi's legs, caressing and teasing and demanding, much as her mouth was doing to nipples. Mimi's release was rapid and powerful.

"Working late certainly agrees with you," she whispered into Gianna's ear. Still straddling her, she rotated her hips gently

133

against Gianna's hand.

"I was thinking about you all night."

"Is that how the son of the Auld Sod got the drop on you? You were mooning over me...ouch!"

Gianna bit her shoulder, then kissed the place. "I wouldn't have the son of a...the son of the sod, had it not been for you. I thank you and Eric thanks you and his excellency the chief thanks you."

"You told him how you found out where they were?"

"Of course I told him. Since he hadn't issued me a crystal ball to gaze into, I had to come up with Florida somehow, not to mention the description of the van and guys inside....and oh, get this." And she told Mimi about the hole in the bottom of the truck and how the sixth man crawled out of it, under Eric's truck, and was half way through the New York Avenue tunnel before he was spotted. And she told her about Lieutenant Gomez's comments, which drew a frown and, Gianna could see, concerns similar to her own.

"What do you think he meant?" Mimi asked.

Gianna shook her head. "I don't have a clue and I really don't want to think about it tonight." She released Mimi and reached around to the tray of food. "Hungry?"

"What are we talking about?" Mimi asked.

"It's a good thing tomorrow's Satur...today. Today's Saturday. It's almost time to get up!" Gianna exclaimed.

"Given what that crazy ass Irishman did to your body, and what I plan to do, you won't be getting up until Sunday, Lieutenant. Now here," she said, giving Gianna her drink.

"I only wish I could sleep until Sunday. Talk about being thankful for small favors, my first appointment isn't until one tomor...*this* afternoon. And that's only because she's a musician and a night owl."

"Anybody I know?"

Gianna hesitated. "Peggy Carter, the *Bayou* singer."

"How's it going?" Mimi asked.

Gianna swallowed a big gulp of vodka and sighed as the warmth spread through her body. "Well, now that I'm done babysitting gun runners and drug dealers, perhaps I can do more than pay lip service to working the thing."

"Do you know why the chief..."

"I do not, and I do not want to talk about the Chief of Police right now. That would upset me and I don't want to be upset. I want to be with you and I want to know what's going on with you these days. How's your story shaping up?"

"Do you really care?"

"What a shitty thing to say!" Gianna gave Mimi a not-so-gentle shove that landed her, with a splash, on her butt on the hot tub bench. "Of course I care, Mimi, how could you say something so...so....mean?"

"You hung up on me when you found out that I'd talked to Renee about Millie Cartcher, and--"

"I shouldn't have done that and I'm sorry. And while I won't apologize for the fact that I don't like it when we end up on the same case, it doesn't mean that I don't care about what you're doing, Mimi, or that I don't wish you well."

Mimi turned sideways to face her. "Really?"

"Yes, really."

"OK. The story I'm working on is only superficially about Millie Cartcher and Ellie Litton. The focus is on how we view and treat women of a certain age in our society, and how if the society didn't make them feel like their lives ended on their fiftieth birthdays, then maybe Millie and Ellie would still be alive....why are you looking at me like that?"

"What do you know about Ellie Litton?"

Mimi groaned. "Oh, Lord, here we go again."

Peggy Carter lived in a four-story, Federal-front townhouse on the edge of Georgetown that had belonged to her parents back when Georgetown was a Black neighborhood. Georgetown now was the most exclusive enclave in D.C. and its narrow, cobblestone streets never held enough parking, a fact that always made Gianna question the nature of exclusivity. Thanks to a layer of sand, courtesy of the Department of Sanitation, and the blindingly bright sunlight, much of the ice had melted or the street would have been impassable. When Gianna got to Peggy's house, she was standing in the door directing the efforts of a man who was trying to break up and remove the ice glazing the front steps; the walkway was cleared. Gianna put her shield in the window, parked in a **WEATHER EMERGENCY NO PARKING** zone, and got out of the car.

Peggy called out that Gianna should enter the house via the basement door, which was beneath the steps, invisible from the street. Virtually all of the old row houses had separate entrances for what once had been servants' quarters and which very often now were rental units. Gianna caught the keys Peggy tossed her and opened first the iron gate and then the metal-enforced door. Once inside, it was clear that the space was, in fact, an unoccupied rental unit. It was large, open and surprisingly bright, with hardwood floors and white plaster walls, devoid of ornamentation. An alcove at the far end of the room contained a sink, stove and refrigerator, and Gianna imagined that through the passageway off to her right there was a bathroom and an exit to the back yard. She started up the steps and heard deadbolts being turned.

"I'm so sorry you had to come in this way," Peggy Carter exclaimed as Gianna moved past her into a hallway as lushly appointed as the downstairs was stark. Framed photographs spanning most of the last century created a gallery in the hall, and thick Persian carpets reflected blue and red and gold in the chandelier's crystal.

"No apology necessary," Gianna said, shaking hands with Peggy. "If we'd scheduled our appointment for an hour later, the sun would have done the work for you." And she followed Peggy up the hall and into what once was called a parlor and what now was a combination den-music room. The center piece was a concert quality grand piano. The other element Gianna noticed was the crackling fire. As she claimed a wing chair opposite Peggy's in front of the fireplace, she noticed a television and VCR, a stereo and CD player, and wall of bookshelves, full from top to bottom, and dozens more photographs. And the room, despite its elegance, was one of the most comfortable she'd ever been in. Comfortable like Peggy Carter was comfortable; elegant like Peggy Carter was elegant, though she was different in her home. Gone were the high fashion wig and sequined gown and stiletto heels and movie star make-up. Her short hair was shot through with silver. She wore a black wool jump suit and fuzzy slippers and only the barest hint of lipstick.

"I'm going to run back into the kitchen in a minute," Peggy told her. "The coffee and muffins should be ready. I just got up and I'm hungry. Hope you are, too."

Gianna was, and spent the next hour eating orange bran muffins and listening to Peggy Carter talk about a way of life that existed only in the memories of people like herself. She was, she said, sixty years old and a classically trained pianist. Her parents, both physicians whom she described as "very proper Negroes of their day," were heartbroken at her decision to pursue the life of a jazz musician. "But they were more devastated to learn that I was a lesbian. That simply was not an option for a girl like me, in that time and place." She still looked and sounded sad, as if the confrontation with her parents had occurred just recently instead of, as best Gianna could tell, more than forty years ago.

"I had to admit they were right about life as a jazz musician. Not only was it no life for a woman, it was no life for a human being." Her posture sagged a bit as she looked into another past— not the life of privilege that she lived with her parents, but the life on the road, never eating or sleeping properly or enough; never receiving the acclaim she sought. "Since I had degrees in music and since it was too late for that concert career, I started teaching music to support myself, and I've been doing that ever since."

"How did you come to be at *The Bayou?*" Gianna had taken out her pen and notebook and the micro cassette tape recorder that she often used to record interviews.

"Through a friend, Jackie Marshall. She's one of the new owners of the place up in Maryland, *Happy Landings.*"

"You mean Marianne and Renee's old place?"

Peggy nodded. "Jackie was my first lover— I met her at a jazz club over near Howard University that's long gone. God, we were young! We've remained friends over the years. She's one of the heirs to a Maryland tobacco plantation and we had some good laughs over the unlikelihood of our union."

"I'll bet you did, though it couldn't have been all laughs. It must have been painful, too."

"Oh, it was that, for sure, but we kept each other from letting the pain get to be too bad. But you didn't come here to listen to war stories, you want to talk about Sandy. What do you want to know? I only talked to her a few times but I think I got to know her pretty well."

"A few times? More than once?"

"Yes. At least a dozen times, maybe more."

"I was under the impression that Sandy had been into *The Bayou* just the one time, the night she was killed."

Peggy was shaking her head. "I don't know where you got that idea. Maybe nobody saw her the other times— she always came straight into the lounge. She came to see me." She faltered on the words and tears welled in her eyes.

"Peggy, if there's a beginning to this story, could you start there and tell it all to me? Please?"

On Sandy's first visit to *The Bayou* she had rushed weeping into the lounge where Peggy, alone, was rehearsing. It was early afternoon and the club was closed to the public and both women were surprised at the presence of the other. Before Sandy could rush out Peggy caught her, consoled and comforted and quieted her, and learned that she'd just had a major argument with her lover. She also learned that Sandy, who had arrived in D.C. that very day, already was regretting the decision. It had become instantly clear that the new lover was, in Sandy's words, a control freak with a violent temper. "She wanted Sandy to live out in the countryside somewhere, in Columbia or Reston. Sandy had lived in small, college towns all her life and even though the idea of living in a city like Washington terrified her, she was also excited. To keep the peace she had said she would live in Maryland, but she rented an apartment on Capitol Hill. She also was going to be teaching at Howard in January, not at Morgan State, as ordered," Peggy said, not trying to hide the bitterness.

"You said 'ordered?'"

"That's right. She *ordered*, commanded, that Sandy do as she said. She claimed she wanted to protect her, to keep her safe. She even bought all of Sandy's furniture and a whole new wardrobe! Can you imagine? She wanted Sandy to have all new clothes in her presence. That's worse than a control freak, don't you think, Lieutenant?"

Gianna didn't know what to think. "So you and Sandy became... close?"

Peggy wiped her eyes again. "Not like that. We were never intimate, not physically, but we talked for hours on end, about everything. And I hoped...wished....allowed myself to believe that when Sandy finally worked through her problems with Trudi, she and I could build something together."

"Trudi the bartender?"

"The very one."

Peggy's bitter words hung there between them while they watched the fire dance and crackle, while Gianna tried to remember every piece of information that existed in the files about Trudi. The only detail that would come to mind was that Trudi also had worked at *Happy Landings* and that she lived in Columbia. And that she'd never mentioned having known the murder victim.

"How did she meet Trudi, Peggy, do you know?

"On the internet, in one of those chat rooms, of all places.

I know first hand how lonely life can be, but in a chat room! You don't know *who* it is you're talking to! I've got several friends, though, who swear it's a great way to meet people."

"And they've had good experiences?"

That seemed to brighten Peggy a bit. "Depends on what you mean by 'good,' doesn't it? None of the chat dates have ever been who they said they were, but then, most of us aren't who we say we are, you know? But what I do know about Sandy Phillips is that she never said— or wrote— a single word that would let somebody believe that she could be ordered or commanded to do *anything.*"

"Let me get this straight: Sandy came to D.C. to be with Trudi, only Trudi thought that Sandy was going to live in Columbia? And teach in Baltimore? And when she learned the truth, she became angry? And what? Threatened Sandy?"

"She hit her."

"Trudi hit Sandy? When?"

"That first day when she came into the lounge crying."

"Peggy, does Trudi or anybody else here know about the relationship between you and Sandra?"

Peggy shook her head vehemently. "No! We didn't want that, either of us, because it would just get the dirt flying. That's why there was no relationship. There was the beginning of a good friendship and as far as anybody knew she came into the lounge because she liked the music. But we didn't give any reason for gossip. Except for that first time, all of our conversations took place on the telephone or at the American Cafe on Capitol Hill, near where Sandy lived. We never talked when she came here. In fact, as soon as I played my signature song, she'd leave."

"What song was that?"

"*Love Letters.* You remember the Ketty Lester hit...no, you don't, do you? You're too young for that," she said, getting up and walking over to the piano. She sat down and lifted the cover and touched the keys and the dark, rich, sweet sound spilled out of the instrument. Six chords. Then Peggy's voice, darker, richer, sweeter than the notes from the piano. *Love letters straight from your heart..*

Gianna had heard the song, though as an adult; and now, listening to it, wished she had been young and in love the first time she'd heard it. She could easily imagine shy, reserved Sandy, disillusioned and saddened by her experience with Trudi, falling in love with the elegant, talented Peggy as she sang that song.

Too much was happening in Gianna's head at once, too many questions, too many images, too many unconnected bits and pieces of information, too many possibilities. She slowed down her brain activity as Peggy resumed her seat in front of the fire and poured more coffee.

"Did Marianne and Renee know about Trudi and Sandy?"

"No indeed, Trudi wouldn't have that. That's why she didn't want Sandy to come in the bar, why she wanted her to live and work out in the 'burbs. She's supposed to be Madam Stud, you know, women swooning at the sight of her and falling at her feet. It wouldn't do for her to have a girlfriend, especially an old one." And finally Peggy broke. She didn't try to stop or conceal the tears. She let them fall freely and they made dark spots like blood on her shirt front. "I thought I had been given one last chance at love. Sandy was a wonderful woman, Lieutenant. She was smart and funny and beautiful and loving and giving....her mother! Have you talked to her mother?"

"I haven't personally but one of our investigators has." The investigator whose report should be on her desk within the next few hours. "Why do you ask?"

"Would you do something for me, Lieutenant? Would you please make sure that Sandy's mother gets the necklace back?"

Gianna called up Sandra Phillips's autopsy report in her memory. There was no mention of a necklace. No mention of jewelry of any kind, she told Peggy.

"Then something's very wrong. She never took off that necklace. It was a gold Star of David on a chain. I asked her why a

141

Black woman was wearing a Star of David. She told me that her parents worked for a Jewish family— her father as chauffeur, her mother as housekeeper— and when they retired after more than thirty years in that house, raising those children and cooking their meals, that was the family's gift to them. Instead of being angry or bitter, Sandy wore it as a reminder of her parents' gift to her. She was the first college graduate in her family. On the salaries of a chauffeur and a housekeeper, she went to college and graduate school. That's why she wore that necklace and that's why she never took it off and if it wasn't on her, then whoever killed her took it. You find that necklace, you'll find Sandy's killer."

"What do you mean Trudi's not here today?" Gianna's anger was unbridled and Marianne flinched and backed up a step. "I made the appointment to talk to her and the other staff through you on Thursday afternoon. It is now Saturday afternoon, less than forty-eight hours later, and you're telling me she's off this weekend? When exactly did that come about, Marianne, and why didn't you tell me about it?"

"Since when do I have to tell you about my staffing decisions? This is *my* private property, not--"

"This is the last place a murder victim was seen alive, a murder victim who had been here a half dozen times, not just the one time, as I've been led to believe. I want her personnel file and I want it now and I want to talk to the rest of the staff. Unless they're all off, too."

Marianne was shocked and frightened and Gianna didn't give the tiniest damn about her feelings as she watched her scurry off. She was furious with herself for not having scheduled the interviews with the club staff sooner, furious with the chief at having had her waste so much time and effort and personnel chasing down the Irish nationals and their guns. For as much as she sympathized with his dilemma, she hadn't liked the feeling of being a pawn in some City Hall chess game while a possible serial killer slipped through her fingers, and she stilled the voice of

142

reason inside herself warning that she had no proof, nothing to back up her suspicion that Trudi the bartender was a serial killer.

Taking her cell phone from her purse and thankful that it still held a charge despite her failure to charge it overnight, she called the Think Tank, unsure who would be there, and gratified to hear Alice Long on the other end. She told Alice what she needed, ended the call, punched in Eric's number, spoke briefly, and clicked off the phone. No use taxing what was left of the battery, and no use being annoyed at having to wait— for Trudi's personnel file from Marianne and for Alice to arrive. She closed her eyes and replayed her conversation with Peggy. The woman had told her a lot. She had no way of knowing how much of it could have any bearing on the case, but she intended to follow up on every name of every person and place Peggy had mentioned. She dropped down into a chair at one of the tables and winced at the effort. Her mind had been so otherwise occupied that she'd forgotten how stiff and sore she was from last night's middle-of-the-street tussle with the Irish gangster. The stiff soreness would only get worse as the day wore on, which was why she'd agreed to meet Mimi at the gym later for a sauna and a massage. An appointment she would not be able to keep.

Marianne returned with a lavender file folder which she held out to Gianna. "Just for the record, I didn't know that the dead...that Sandra Phillips had been here more than the one time. For God's sake, Gianna, I'd never have kept that from you, and you should know that."

"Why did Trudi come to work here? If she still lives in Columbia, why didn't she stay at *Happy Landings?*

"She doesn't get along with Erin and Jackie, the new owners. She asked if she could come here and I said sure. She's good at her job and she'd make much more in tips here because she's so popular with the women. Listen, Gianna..."

"When did you find out that Trudi wouldn't be here today?"

Marianne gave Gianna a long, cold look before she replied

that Trudi had called at seven that morning to say she'd slipped on the ice last night and twisted her ankle, which was sore and swollen, and she needed a couple of days to rest it. She'd be back in time for the Monday staff meeting. Gianna cursed. Another forty-eight hours without access to her prime suspect and not a single shred of evidence to justify requesting surveillance or a search warrant. All other evidence notwithstanding, a lie was not evidence; it was proof of nothing. She cursed again and Marianne shrugged and walked away and Gianna thought it was just as well that her friend was angry with her. It was a good place to start from, anger, when the only place left to go was into rage.

Gianna called her name and Marianne turned around. Gianna walked over to her. "I need to know everything you know about Trudi. How long you've known her, what you know about her family and her friends and her lovers, everything, Marianne, no matter how insignificant you think it might be."

"You think she had something to do with the murder?"

"What I think matters less than what I know, and what I know is that Trudi worked at *Happy Landings* and now she works here, and that three of the victims are known to have frequented both places. Both places owned by you and both places where Trudi worked. That's what I know. What I don't know is where the connection is, but believe me I will know before I leave here today and you, Marianne, will either be part of the problem or part of the solution. The choice is yours."

"You're a cold one, Gianna."

Gianna nodded. It wasn't the first time she'd heard that assessment of herself, and it probably wouldn't be the last.

144

CHAPTER TEN

Mimi was into her fourth mile on the treadmill and sweating profusely when the gym's manager came to tell her that Gianna wouldn't be joining her, that "there had been a development." She nodded her thanks and pressed the buttons to slow the machine to a brisk walk while she wondered what the "development" was. They had had a very frank and open talk the previous night after Gianna had recovered from the fact that Mimi knew about Ellie Litton and Mimi had explained how. Had the talk been open and frank enough that Gianna would tell her what the development was?

The treadmill stopped and she stepped off, deep in thought. Gianna said that when she could, she'd tell Mimi how and why Millie and Ellie had died. Mimi had said she was interested in the other victim only to the extent that their deaths, too, were related to their ages. With that information Mimi thought she could build a hell of a series on how society's treatment of women in general, and older women in particular, fostered a dangerous self-destruction within the largest segment of the population. All she needed for the story were real women, some who were still alive and who would talk openly about how they felt about being at this turning point in their lives.

"What are you thinking about so intensely?"

Mimi turned to see Phyllis smiling at her. "As a matter of fact I was thinking about you," she said, returning the smile. "How's the workout? And where's the rest of your crew?"

She followed Phyllis's glance across the room and Evie, June and Dot waved at her. Then Phyllis turned back to Mimi. "That was either a very nice thing to say, or a very cruel one."

"I meant no cruelty, Phyllis, and I *was* thinking of you— the four of you— and wishing I knew how to contact you." And she explained why.

145

"You want to put us in the paper so the world can laugh at us by name instead of just some old, fat women?"

Mimi was annoyed with Phyllis and let her know it. "How is it— *why* is it that you heard the exact opposite of what I said to you? And this is why I want to do the story, to dispel the negative images, including those you yourself hold, and to embrace all that's good and positive about you."

Phyllis snorted. "When was the last time you embraced a fifty-something year old woman? And the fact that you were wondering how to find us means you don't even know any, 'cause if you did, you'd ask them."

And she stalked off, leaving Mimi feeling bad in a new and different way. Because, she realized, Phyllis was right. Aside from Kate and Sue and their friends whom she'd met in Florida, she didn't know, as friends, any women older than herself. Why was that? Could it be because, like the culture at large, she held older women in lower esteem? Then she brightened as she realized that with the exception of Gianna, Beverly and Sylvia, and Freddie and Cedric, she didn't have any other close friends of *any* age.

She looked across the room at the four women who were looking back at her. She took a deep breath and headed for them.

"I told you to leave us alone," Phyllis hissed.

"Are you M. Montgomery Patterson?" Evie asked

"I am," Mimi said.

"I've probably read every story you've written and I can't believe you'd write the kind of thing Phyllis just told us about. That's not even close to the kind of stuff you do. That doesn't sound like your kind of story."

"It's not," Mimi said, and she explained with more detail, the story she wanted to write.

"Who do you think wants to read anything about women over fifty?" Dot asked. "Since you already know how we're perceived and treated, who's going to read your articles?"

"If *only* women over fifty read the stories that would be

more than half the population. But I think women my age will be interested because I think they'll feel the same way I did when I understood what peri-menopause meant. It gives me the night sweats just to think about it, and it's the middle of the afternoon."

"You know about night sweats?" Dot asked.

"More than I care to," Mimi said, "and more than my fifty-something friends got around to mentioning to me."

June grinned and Evie's face relaxed out of its scowl.

"You don't know anybody over fifty, remember?" Phyllis was still angry.

"Actually, I do, but they live in Florida. Made a killing in the tech market before it crashed, quit their government jobs, and moved to the land of permanent sun."

"I took a beating in the tech market and will have to keep my government job for at least another eight years, until I'm sixty-two," Evie said, looking for the moment as sorrowful as she sounded.

"But if you got to know us, you'd be friends with us?" There was challenge in Phyllis's voice .

"Of course," Mimi replied, "assuming we had enough things in common to warrant building a friendship."

"I'm a lawyer at the Justice Department," said June, "and I know lots of secrets. Is that basis for a friendship?"

Mimi shook her head. "I'd never have a source as a friend or use a friend as a source."

"But you want to put us in your story," Phyllis wailed.

Mimi reached out to the woman and put an arm around her shoulders. Phyllis collapsed into her and Mimi was overwhelmed at the pain she could feel transmitted, pain born of shame, the shame due only to the fact of lost youth. "I won't use any of your names, if that's what you wish, but I need the benefit of your knowledge, of your thoughts and feelings and experiences. Everything that comes with having reached a certain age. And I need to hear those things from some women who don't feel as if something terrible happened on their fiftieth birthday. There must be women who are happy and thriving and looking forward to every birthday the way we did when were thirteen and twenty-three and thirty-three. And I need to know whether more open and public and frank and honest talk about what menopause is and does would have made a difference in your lives and how you feel about yourselves."

The four women exchanged glances, then studied Mimi for several seconds.

"I think she's got potential," Dot said. "Shall we invite her?"

June nodded, and waited for the others to follow suit. Phyllis reluctantly added her assent, and it was she who explained that this was their game night. More than twenty of them—women who'd been friends since college, some straight, some gay— gathered one Saturday night a month to play card games and board games and to laugh and talk and enjoy the freedom to be silly. "But you can't interrogate people," Phyllis said. "You can't make them uncomfortable."

"And bring your girlfriend," Evie said. "You do have one, don't you?"

Mimi nodded. "I'll bring her if she's not working." But she knew Gianna would be working. Whatever had "developed" between last night and this afternoon wouldn't be resolved by seven o'clock tonight. Then Mimi had another thought. "Can I bring my friends Beverly and Sylvia? I think you'd like them and I think they'd like you and Bev is brilliant at board games."

Gianna sat in the back seat of her unmarked re-reading the field reports of the Missing Persons investigators who had done the home town checks on Sandra Phillips, Millicent Cartcher, Ellie Litton and Mabel Gunther. Kenny drove and Linda rode shotgun, walking the Boss through the reports which she'd already read and digested and dissected, directing Gianna's attention to the most salient points, including the fact that every body who'd ever known the victims described them as intelligent, good, kind, decent women, without exception. They were known to be hard-working, accomplished, even. And with the exception of Millie Cartcher, not a single friend or family member of any of the victims had had any notion that the women were lesbians. Sandra Phillips's mother had suspected but she hadn't known for certain. The other families had had no clue. And if the women had ever had intimate relations with anyone in their hometowns, either nobody knew it or those who knew weren't telling, even in death. And there was another point of agreement: Each of the victims wore a piece of jewelry her family said she never removed. Sandy Phillips had her Star of David. Ellie Litton wore her brother Elvis's high school class ring on the baby finger of her left hand. Millie Cartcher affixed to every outfit a brooch that had belonged to the great-grandmother for whom she was named. Mabel Gunther wore a toe ring on her left foot, a gift from a woman she called sister who lived in Nigeria. None of these pieces of jewelry was mentioned in the police report or in the autopsy report.

"You find that necklace, you'll find Sandy's killer."

Gianna's stomach growled and she looked at her watch; all she'd had to eat that day were Peggy Carter's orange bran muffins. Peggy Carter, whose voice still resonated in her ears. *You find that necklace, you'll find Sandy's killer. A last chance at love.* Somebody else had said that. Who was it? She replayed the phrase in her memory and heard, along with Peggy's voice, Alice Long's. It's what Alice said that Mabel had said. *A last chance at love.*

It was almost dark and even within the car with the heater blasting Gianna could feel the frigid air that had descended upon the region earlier in the day, the kind of cold that would linger a few days, and that would penetrate. She was glad she'd put on the silk tights and long sleeve undershirt beneath her lined wool slacks and wool-blend sweater. She was glad she'd worn boots with inch thick soles instead of regular street shoes. She was glad she'd allowed Kenny and Linda to pick her up from *The Bayou.* She'd gotten all she was going to get from the people there. If

149

there was anything else to get, Alice could get it. She wasn't hated. Yet. And perhaps by the time a killer was caught, Gianna wouldn't be, either.

"Why are we stopping, Kenny?"

"Dinner, Boss."

"Oh. Right. Do you need money?"

"Detective Ashby gave me money."

Gianna looked out the window and was surprised to find they were in Chinatown, just blocks from the office, in front of the restaurant that was their favorite. Their arrival was expected because before Kenny could open the car door, two white-jacketed delivery guys were running down the steps, their arms full of brown bags. Linda reached behind her and opened the back door and the men piled the food in. "Eric must really be hungry," she said when Kenny had paid for the food and they'd driven away.

"He said you'd really be hungry."

"Yeah," she said, "he's right, I am, but this is an awful lot of food."

And an hour later it all was gone and the eight of them— Gianna, Eric, Tim, Kenny, Linda, Cassie, Bobby and Alice— were elbow deep in case files, autopsy reports, field reports, and evidence check-off forms, the Hate Crimes Team's own private evidence assessment sheet. They'd all had a hand in devising the form to help them keep up with the myriad bits and pieces of information that accumulate during investigations of serial murders, of which they'd had two prior to the current one.

That the current murders were the work of the same killer, there could be no doubt. That the victims were all lesbians also was practically accepted as fact. Every victim was between the ages of fifty and sixty— and thanks to the missing person investigators they had exact birth dates for all the women they had identified. There still were two Jane Does, dead the longest, and who, without help from the killer, were likely to remain so. A good reason by itself for nailing this perp.

All of the victims had been dressed in new clothing, head

to toe and underwear to top coat. None of the victims wore any jewelry. All of the women were from small towns, and all died within several months of moving to the Washington area. And with the exception of Sandra Phillips, all of the women would be considered plain, if not homely.

"I think that's significant," Cassie Ali said. "That and the fact that she was here only a few weeks instead of a few months. I think those two things are related."

"Me, too," echoed Tim McCreedy, "though I'm not sure why."

"Because they're the only two differences among all the similarities," Linda Lopez said, and looked toward Gianna. "Right, Boss?"

"None of them left money in their hometown banks," Gianna said, her mind following a train of thought. "And their bank accounts here were cleaned out within days of their deaths." Something Mimi said the previous night re-kindled a thought she'd toyed with. Greed as a motive. Mimi told her that when she first learned of Millicent Cartcher's murder, her instinct had been to follow the money. That was Gianna's current instinct. All the new things the victims possessed— houses, clothes, furniture, cars— and the missing jewelry and the looted bank accounts and the secrecy. They all pointed to greed as a motive. And to a narcissistic personality.

"Who's got Millie?" Gianna asked.

"Me," said Bobby, pulling the pages of his file together in front of him.

"And who's got Marianne?"

Kenny gathered his file and looked expectantly at Gianna.

"Millie's at *Happy Landings* on the first warm, spring day." She stopped and waited for Bobby and Kenny to find that fact in their files.

"She's sitting outside in the garden--"

"And Marianne says she took her drink to her--"

"Then," Gianna said, "Millie was left outside alone..."

Bobby turned some pages. "For about an hour..."

"And Marianne said she went back out to check on her." Gianna leaned back in her chair, put her feet on the desk, crossed her ankles, and closed her eyes. "And found her kissing a woman she didn't know, someone she'd never seen before. Tall, curly dark hair, glasses."

There was no sound in the room, no movement. Six pairs of eyes sought Gianna's, which remained closed. They shared glances with each other; wary, confused glances. Then, gradually, looks of surprise and something like dismay.

"Fuck a duck," Bobby whispered.

"Unless she's lying...unless Marianne is flat-out lying to us about what the woman looked like..." said Tim.

"It wasn't Trudi Millie was kissing," said Linda.

"Oh, shit," Cassie said.

"Then there's two of 'em? Is that what this means?"

"Either there's two of 'em or Trudi's not in it at all."

"Fuck a duck," Bobby said again.

Gianna opened her eyes, dropped her chair to the floor, stood up, and took off her jacket. She stretched her back, did a deep knee bend, and sat back down at the table. "Let's take it from the top, people," she said.

Mimi awoke much too early Sunday morning but since staying in bed alone was no fun, she got up and made coffee and read the paper, and went back to bed. She got up again at noon, drank more coffee, ate oatmeal and toast, and was contemplating spending the rest of the day in bed when the phone rang. She snatched it up, hoping it was Gianna. She'd worked all night and maybe she finally was home. It was Beverly calling to say that she and Sylvia had had a great time the previous night, and she thanked Mimi for inviting them.

Mimi herself had had a great time with Phyllis and Dot and June and Evie and their friends. If any of the twenty-six women there ever experienced any loneliness or sadness or resentment at the fact of their ages, none of it was present last night. They had laughed and giggled, danced and played, talked and sung, like having fun was the most important thing they did with their lives. They were raucous and raunchy and funny. And they were caring and loving and generous. They were all shapes and sizes and colors and as far as Mimi was concerned, not a single one of them should ever have to worry about being loved. The phone rang again and it was Phyllis. She thanked Mimi for bringing Beverly and Sylvia to the party and hinted that she might be willing to give Mimi a chance at friendship after all.

Mimi hung up feeling refreshed and energized and no longer wanting to spend the rest of the day in bed. The wind howled outside, rattling the windows and momentarily halting any desire to go out. Her annual cord of firewood hadn't been delivered yet but she had a few sticks of kindling and several fake logs left. So, instead of spending the day in bed, she could spend it in front of the fireplace...at *Happy Landings*.

Erin's welcome was somewhat less than warm but she was willing to hear and accept Mimi's apology for the other day. Until Mimi more fully identified herself and her reason for being there.

"Of all the nerve!" Erin's exclamation was loud enough that every head in the bar turned toward them and a woman whom Mimi surmised was Erin's mother rushed in from the kitchen, concern etched in her face.

"What's the trouble?" she exclaimed, looking worriedly from Erin to Mimi. She was a gorgeous woman— five-six or seven, hair completely silver and cut close, eyes clear and hazel like Gianna's and, like Gianna, had a way of claiming attention with a gaze. So Mimi gazed and upon closer inspection, realized there was no resemblance whatever to Erin. They possessed different kinds of beauty.

"It seems that almost everything I say upsets Erin and I'm really sorry about that. It's not my intention. I'm Montgomery Patterson," she said extending her hand.

153

"M. Montgomery Patterson, the reporter?" The woman shook Mimi's hand.

"The one who was in here the other day, the one I told you about. And I told you she was lying."

"I didn't lie to you," Mimi said. "I never got around to telling you I was a reporter because I never could seem to say anything that didn't piss you off. But I never once lied to you."

The color was high in Erin's face. "You said you weren't straight."

"And I'm not."

"You said you didn't know that other woman."

"And I didn't. Had never seen her in my life until she walked in your door."

Erin looked at the woman standing next to her, then back at Mimi, then she turned and stalked away.

"I'm Jackie Marshall. Erin's my partner in life, love and business. Her hot head is one of her many endearing qualities."

"I'm truly sorry to have offended her," Mimi said, hoping she had covered her surprise at Jackie's revelation. "It's not my policy to mislead people about who I am and what I'm doing."

"And what are you doing?"

Mimi told her.

Jackie laughed. "I could easily have killed a few people when I was in the throes of menopause, but I think I was too mean and nasty to have stood still long enough for anybody to have gotten close enough to kill me." She fixed Mimi in her hazel gaze. "They're going to let you do a story on *menopause?*"

Mimi tried again to explain. "It's not *on* menopause so much as it's about why something so completely normal and natural is misunderstood to the point of having been demonized." She sighed dejectedly. "I'm really not doing such a good job of explaining this, am I? Maybe there's no story there."

"I think the fact that it is so difficult to explain something so ancient and so pervasive and so natural and normal means there's a hell of a story there," Jackie said. Then she became still and silent and when she spoke again it was at length about how she came to be with Erin and, ultimately, the co-owner of a bar. "She didn't have any real idea how much work was involved. When she worked for her Dad, the men did all the heavy, dirty work and Erin mixed and served drinks and charmed the customers. Even when she worked here she couldn't see all the work Marianne and Renee put in— they practically lived here, just as they're doing with that new place. And now Erin's thinking maybe she made a big mistake. This really is too much for one person."

"But you're here."

"I'm here today, but this is rare. I have my own business to run." Jackie raised her eyes from Mimi's, scanned the room, and then lowered her voice. "Erin's afraid, Miss Patterson, that somebody she knows well has something to do with those murdered women."

"Who is this somebody?" Mimi asked, feeling almost angry that the focus of her story had just shifted and that she'd probably never get it back. She was about to learn the identity of a murderer.

"Her name's Trudi Thompson and she used to be the bartender here."

"And she works at *The Bayou* now, right?" Mimi asked, remembering the play Trudi made for Gianna.

Jackie shook her head. "Not any more. She was at our house early this morning saying that Marianne had fired her and begging Erin for a job reference. She said she's leaving the area, going to Texas."

"Did you call the police?"

"For what?" Jackie exclaimed.

Mimi willed herself to remain calm. "You said you think Trudi knows something about the murders of Millicent Cartcher and Ellie Litton. You also said she's planning to leave town."

"But I don't really *know* anything. I just suspect--"

"And if your suspicions are unfounded, the police will

155

leave Trudi in peace, but they need the chance to make that decision, Miss Marshall. Six women are dead--"

"Six! My God! You said two, you said the Cartcher girl and Ellie Litton!"

"Those are the ones I know about for a fact. The others a police source told me about off the record which means that's information I technically cannot use. But I'm telling you, Miss Marshall, that six women are dead, all killed the same way, and if you think Trudi had anything to do with that, you need to tell the police."

"I can't," she whispered.

Mimi looked into her eyes and saw fear. "You think Erin's involved."

"I don't know. I'm not sure. I think she knows Trudi did something wrong and I think that she may suspect...oh, God, Miss Patterson, I don't know what to do!"

"I told you what to do. Call the police."

"Can you do that for me? Would you? You said you had a police source."

So much for a cozy Sunday in front of the fire. Mimi leaned into the wind, hurrying to her car. She had dressed warmly in tights and a turtleneck beneath wool slacks and a thick, cable knit sweater. She wore hiking boots with thick socks and a sheepskin jacket, and the wind cut through the clothes to slice at her skin as if she were naked. She slid into the car but didn't start the engine, cold though she was. "What a mess," she muttered as she reached for the Thomas Guide maps beneath the seat, and she looked up the address Jackie Marshall had given her for Trudi Thompson. A straight shot down the main road.

She dug around in her purse for her cell phone, pressed the button, and waited for it to let her talk. The message on the screen told her the battery was low before it shut itself off. She threw it into the back seat, started the car, and drove too fast out of the parking lot, catching a patch of ice left over from the other night and skidding slightly before straightening out.

She put the open map on the passenger seat and plotted a route to Trudi Thompson's house, counting on there being a gas station or convenience store or fast food joint en route so she could stop and call Gianna at a pay phone. She imagined that Gianna and her team already knew about Trudi and briefly considered not making the call, but she reminded herself if by some error in the Universe they didn't know and Gianna found out that Mimi had known and not told her, there would be too much hell to pay. Better to call and get a grouch on the phone now than possibly have to deal with a monster later.

Three and a half miles into the drive on a state road that she wished had been better salted and sanded, Mimi turned into a gas-and-go mart and pulled up to a pump. She needed fuel for the car and for herself. The oatmeal and toast had long since worn off, and, she remembered, she'd planned on having a plate of Erin's mother's crab cakes. Her stomach growled at the thought. Maybe a bottle of mineral water and a bag of popcorn would satiate until she got back to D.C. and to Crisfield's, a seafood house that had been on Georgia Avenue in Silver Spring almost since Indians first discovered crabs in the Chesapeake Bay. Her stomach growled again.

She'd paid for the gasoline, water and popcorn and was headed for the door when Trudi Thompson exited the women's restroom at the rear of the store, drying her hands on a paper towel which she crumpled and tossed, as if shooting a basket, into a trash can at the front of the store. She looked to see if the store clerk noticed. He hadn't. She looked at Mimi and something registered in her face.

Mimi walked over to her and introduced herself. "I've seen you at *The Bayou* a couple of times."

"I thought you looked familiar. You got in the way of me talking to that sexy bitch with the pretty eyes. And wasn't that you hiding behind the pillar that night when Marianne was talking to that cop? She didn't see you, but I did."

157

"Guess I failed Undercover 101."

Trudi didn't get the joke. Mimi wasn't surprised. Her initial impression of Trudi had been that she wasn't very bright and a closer encounter confirmed that first impression. She was also every bit as attractive as Mimi had recalled though in a smarmy kind of way. The hair was just a bit too blonde and contrived to fall just a bit too carefully over her left eye, but it was thick and curly and you couldn't buy that in a bottle. The deep blue eyes were contact lenses. And though her skin was clear there was the kind of underlying pallor that suggested debauchery. Her jeans hung enticingly low on her narrow hips, the black tee shirt was tight and tucked in, and the black leather jacket hung open to reveal breasts nicely unencumbered by a bra. Mimi thought it was too cold to be concerned about looking sexy but given Trudi's Nordic appearance, maybe she was from Minnesota and wasn't cold.

"What are you doing way out here, city girl?"

"I just left Jackie Marshall's place. She and Erin were helping me with some information, and now that I think about it, maybe you can, too."

"That bitch! What did she tell you?"

All of Mimi's senses were on alert. "I'm working on a story about crime in major metropolitan areas and I'm using a woman named Millie Cartcher, a veterinarian who was from Georgia, as my focus. Her family says she'd still be alive if she'd stayed in Georgia."

"What the hell does this have to do with me?"

"You knew her before you started working in D.C. She used to frequent *Happy Landings*. She was in her mid-fifties..."

"They're all in their mid-fifties. Old bitches, drink too much, got nobody to love 'em, and think if they buy me a couple of drinks it's worth a fuck."

Mimi looked her up and down— a bit of a strain on the up, for Trudi was at least five- nine or ten. She'd be one hell of an attractive package if it weren't for the ugly persona that radiated

158

out from her in all directions. "Is it?"

Trudi returned the gesture, taking a longer time of it. "For you? Yeah." She peered into the bag Mimi carried. "Got any beer in there?"

Mimi shook her head. "I'm driving and I'm not real sure of this road."

Trudi draped an arm across Mimi's shoulders. "Well, I know this road like the back of my hand. I live on it and I'm going home and I'm taking you with me and the beer's already there. That your car? Good, 'cause I wrecked the shit outta mine last night and it's too cold to walk."

Mimi knew from the map where Trudi lived, not necessarily far, but the road was dotted with ice and it was freezing. "How'd you get here?"

"Got a ride, then got dumped. Women suck, present company excepted," she said, drawing Mimi in close to her body. "What say we spend the afternoon talking about what it is *you* want to talk about, then spend the night talking about what it is *I* want to talk about?"

Mimi pushed against Trudi to free herself and the other woman's arm became a steel vise around her shoulders. She dropped her bag and put both hands up to push but Trudi grabbed her arm and twisted, bringing Mimi flush against her.

"Trudi, you take that dyke shit outta my store," the clerk yelled out. "And you, lady, pump your gas and move your car outta the way."

Still gripping Mimi's arm, Trudi picked up the bag with her other hand and propelled Mimi out of the warmth of the store, into the frigid, howling wind.

159

CHAPTER ELEVEN

Gianna's fight with the chief left her drained. Two nights with no sleep and an inability to locate Mimi rendered her too weak for battle, but she had no choice in the matter. She needed his involvement if she was to obtain warrants to search Trudi Thompson's person, house, car, computer, garage, and anything else she owned in Frederick or in any other Maryland county, including her family's home on the Eastern Shore. And she wanted that court order right now. She had suspected that Trudi wouldn't be showing up for work today and a call from Marianne confirmed her worst suspicions. Trudi had quit and she asked Marianne to mail her final paycheck to her mother in Cambridge, Maryland. Marianne was so sorry; seemed that Gianna was right. Seemed that Marianne had had a killer right under her nose and hadn't been able to stop her. Those women dead and Marianne could have done something...

She could have done nothing, Gianna tried to tell her, except most likely put herself and Renee in danger. Not your fault, Gianna told her, and by the way, what are the last names of Erin and Jackie, the women who bought *Happy Landings* from you? Erin Hill and Jackie Marshall. Peggy Carter's first lover. And once again, who was Millie Cartcher kissing that day on the patio? A stranger, yes, but what kind of stranger? Tell me again exactly what she looked like.

Eric, Bobby and Kenny waited in the Think Tank for word from on high that they had their court order and their warrants. Then, joined by Tony Watkins and whatever back-up the chief would provide, they'd get to Columbia as fast as they could and, with the assistance of the local authorities, they'd take apart Trudi Thompson's life. And Trudi Thompson, if they could find her. Alice and Cassie were at *The Bayou* and would remain there until there was no further danger to Marianne or Renee or Peggy Carter. Tim was driving Gianna and Linda, first to Erin and Jackie's home— the bar wouldn't be open this early— and then to sit in front of Trudi's house until the paperwork arrived.

Gianna stretched out in the back seat of the unmarked but didn't sleep. Some of the exhaustion would have to wear off before she could sleep. She sat up, took her cell phone from her bag, and punched in Mimi's numbers again. Home, work, cell phone, the gym. Mimi had left a message yesterday afternoon saying she'd be home by seven at the latest. Gianna had started calling at eight and had called every hour on the hour until the present. She'd even had Eric check accident reports throughout the region in case her too old, too small, classic automobile had skidded off the road and into a tree or down an embankment. Nothing. And Gianna was worried.

Monday morning traffic was dense. Once, in the not so very distant past, Columbia had been woodland. Back then, it was a New Town, like Reston in Virginia, one of those model towns conceived to demonstrate that people of all incomes and races could live in harmony. Then, as it grew, it became a suburb of either Washington or Baltimore, depending on one's residential perspective. And as both Washington and Baltimore expanded, Columbia became extensions of both, so that now, morning and evening, coming and going, traffic around Columbia was dense. Tim was a good driver, an efficient driver, and nobody could make better time. But she wanted him to hurry, to activate lights and siren and cut through all the traffic. But he couldn't. They had no legal authority as cops once they left the Baltimore-Washington Parkway and their own jurisdiction.

She sat up and picked up the sheaf of correspondence between Sandy and Spice. She'd read these pages a dozen times and knew the words and the feelings they conveyed. Sandy's communiqués were letters and her words spoke of hope and excitement at the prospect of nurturing a new love. Spice's offerings were notes— none longer than a paragraph, no sentence longer than a few words— and they all seemed disjointed and disconnected, as if the writer didn't remember what she'd written the previous day. And Spice's words, unlike Sandy's strokes and caresses, spoke of sex and power and subjugation. And Gianna wondered again how Sandy missed the message, even though she knew the answer.

She stuffed the papers back into the folder and looked out at the traffic. The wind had died down overnight and a thick, gray cold had settled over the landscape. Despite the wind, many trees still bore vestiges of fall, and the leaves shivered. Though Tim and Linda had no way of knowing of Gianna's concern for Mimi, concern that was turning to fear, they rode in silence in the front seat, attuned, she knew, to any word or movement on her part that would signal the need for their involvement. But the only thing she needed them to do was get her to Jackie Marshall's front door.

And what a front door it was! Though she knew from Peggy that Jackie was a tobacco heiress, Gianna hadn't given any thought to what, exactly, that might mean in terms of where or how the woman might live. The house facing them at the top of the hill, still a quarter mile away, was wood and fieldstone and looked as if it had lived on top of that hill for a hundred years. A weathered split rail fence led the way to the house and there were horses in a distant field. Smoke curled from chimneys at both ends of the house, which seemed to grow as they got closer. Tim and Linda whistled in unison.

"I think I'm going to open a women's bar," Tim said.

"That would be after you'd raised and sold tobacco for a couple of hundred years," Gianna said, as impressed with the property as they were.

"Guess you'd better keep working on that twenty year pension," Linda said to Tim as he stopped the car to the right of the front door of the house, on the edge of the circular driveway, leaving enough space for another car to pass. There were three other vehicles parked to the left of the door— an ancient though fit-looking Suburban, a middle-aged Blazer that looked as if it had just come from the showroom floor and a three-year old Buick.

The government-issued cop car fit in perfectly.

Gianna was out of the car and up the steps before Tim and Linda got free of their seat belts and they hurried to catch up. She pushed the doorbell and stood squarely in the front door, Tim and Linda flanking her, just out of sight, hands on their weapons. She rang the bell three times before it was answered and knew from Peggy Carter's description who had opened the door; and though she expected that Jackie Marshall would be attractive, she was unprepared the woman's beauty. The two of them— Peggy Carter and Jackie Marshall— must have been quite something together forty years earlier.

"Miss Marshall, I'm Lieutenant Maglione, D.C. Police..."

"Thank God she told you! I worried all night about what to do." Gianna's face must have registered her confusion because Jackie Marshall rushed ahead. "The reporter, didn't she tell you to come here?"

"What reporter, Miss Marshall?"

"Montgomery Patterson. She told me that she had a contact with the police..."

"May we come in, please?"

Jackie Marshall heard the command in Gianna's request and stepped quickly aside to let them enter, and Gianna realized the woman was in her robe and slippers, realized they had awakened her, realized it was Monday and the bar most likely would be closed and that the bar owners most likely would have been sleeping late. Tim and Linda still flanked her but they'd backed slightly away so that they could see down the hallways that branched off from the foyer, while Gianna had a clear view up the wide staircase. What she saw was Erin Hill, yawning and pulling on a robe. Gianna waited for her to descend before she introduced herself again, introduced Officers McCreedy and Lopez, and recovered enough of her wits to ask Jackie Marshall to repeat what she'd said about Montgomery Patterson.

"She was here yesterday— not here at the house, at the bar— and she said she'd tell the police what I told her."

163

"You shouldn't have told her anything, Jackie!" Erin screamed. "Why'd you have to tell her anything? I knew she was nothing but trouble soon as I saw her!"

Gianna gave Erin a look that caused her to flinch and then she looked back at Jackie. "Tell me exactly what you and Montgomery Patterson said to each other, Miss Marshall."

"No, Jackie!" Erin wailed. "Just let it be!

"If you say another word, Miss Hill, I'll have you arrested and charged with obstructing justice and interfering with an officer in the conduct of an investigation. Miss Patterson is missing and so is Trudi Thompson--"

"Trudi said Marianne fired her," Erin interjected. "She's not missing."

"Trudi was not fired and I'm waiting, Miss Marshall," Gianna said.

When Jackie Marshall finished talking, she drew a map with directions to Trudi Thompson's house and she gave written permission for them to use and search her property if necessary, over Erin Hill's objections. Gianna left Linda in the house with explicit instructions not to let Erin Hill out of her sight and she and Tim left the house and returned to the car.

"Drive off the property then find a way to double back and get us to this barn," she said, giving him Jackie Marshall's map and pointing to the barn. "I'd just as soon not be too big a target," she said, the feelings within threatening to overwhelm her. Finally, she thought, there was a real, tangible motive for the killings: Three years ago, young, pretty Erin Hill had left young, pretty Trudi Thompson for the stunning but fifty-seven year old Jackie Marshall. Not only left Trudi but told all their friends and anyone else who would listen that Jackie was superior to Trudi in every way— especially sexually. Virile, studly Trudi, eclipsed and replaced by an "old bitch." She'd threatened to kill them both and had actually cornered Jackie in the parking lot of the Giant Supermarket late one evening and slapped her around. And immediately had felt the weight of what it meant to threaten one

164

of the county's wealthiest, most powerful citizens. It was not a mistake that Trudi would make again; nor was it one that she would live down any time soon. Everywhere she went for the next year, it seemed, somebody knew that she'd been foolish enough, *stupid* enough, to take on a Marshall. Nobody had seen Trudi's action through the lens of Trudi's perspective, which was that she had bravely defended her honor. To the world, Trudi was a fool, a buffoon. And a dyke.

And now, it seemed, Trudi had Mimi in her clutches, for Mimi had left Jackie Marshall the previous afternoon with directions to Trudi Thompson's house and had not been heard from since. The same directions that Gianna now had herself, though she was heading not to Trudi's house but to an abandoned tobacco curing barn on the far edge of the Marshall property where, according to Erin, Trudi and her brother and a female cousin operated an occasional chop shop, an activity and an arrangement that Jackie Marshall had known nothing about until just moments ago when a tearful, apologetic Erin spilled the beans. If Trudi was at home, at the house she shared with her brother and cousin, Eric and the rest of the Team and the backup units with their warrants would find out soon enough. But there would be no warrant to give them permission to search the Marshall estate; there was only Jackie Marshall's written permission. And there was only Gianna and Tim to do it.

Tim pulled the car off the two-lane blacktop and into a clump of trees and underbrush that barely concealed it, but it would have to do. Gianna briefly contemplated and quickly dismissed the thought of calling the chief to tell him what she was doing. He'd order her to wait for legal support and back-up and she didn't have time to wait. Mimi might not have time for her to wait.

She jumped out of the car and slammed the door and Tim followed silently. They stood within the clump of trees and stared into the distance. It was a wide, open field and while it was not exactly flat, there was little protection, either from the elements or from someone witnessing their approach. The barn they were looking for was somewhere out there in that field, and the people they were looking for possibly were in the barn.

"Tim..."

"I'm with you, Boss, all the way."

She nodded and they started across the quasi-soggy land. It hadn't been cold enough long enough to cause a hard freeze, so there were patches of ice interspersed with ankle-deep mud. Both Gianna and Tim wore fleece-lined hunting boots so they managed the terrain without great difficulty. But they knew they were easy targets. They crouched as low as possible and moved as rapidly as possible through the field and the scraggly stalks that scratched, slashed and burned their faces.

Tim stopped suddenly and touched Gianna's arm and pointed to the ground. Tire tracks entering the field from a different direction. Big, deep tracks, from a truck. They turned simultaneously and looked behind them to see where the tracks had begun. They were fresh and they came from a rutted farm road and they led into a stand of trees that rose, incongruously, from the middle of the field, oasis-like. Gianna and Tim took out their weapons, chambered rounds, and crept toward the clump of trees, keeping one eye on the tire tracks and the other on the landscape. They slowed as they reached the trees and, back-to-back, weapons outstretched, they sidled into the thicket. It was like entering a deep forest. It was darker and quieter and much colder. Then Gianna gasped and Tim whirled around to see why. There sat Mimi's 1966 Karmann Ghia, the front end smashed all the way into the back seat. Tim looked his question at Gianna.

"It's Mimi's...Montgomery Patterson's...she's--"

"I know who she is, Boss," Tim whispered before crawling toward the car and looking inside. He couldn't get either of the doors open but he managed to get his head inside, and one arm. He backed out and crawled back to Gianna. "No one inside," he whispered. "And Boss? There's no blood or...or anything. Just this." He gave her the cell phone that Mimi had tossed on the back seat less than twenty-four hours earlier.

Gianna took the phone, punched it on, and saw the low battery message. Willing herself not to react, she punched the phone off, stuck it in her pocket, and they resumed their crawl through the trees. When they emerged they had a direct, clear view of the tobacco curing barn, and anybody in the barn had a direct, clear view of them. They ducked back into the trees.

"We could wait until dark," Tim said.

"We'd freeze to death before it got dark. I'm going to walk up to the door. Tim, you go back the way we came, circle around, and approach from the rear. The element of surprise, such as it may be. I'll give you," she looked at her watch, "fifteen minutes." He started to say something and she waved it off. "Get going, Tim," she ordered, and he loped off, neither crouching nor being especially quiet.

Gianna took Mimi's phone from her pocket and held it close to her face, wanting to capture Mimi's scent. But it was cold. She stashed the phone in her pocket and walked over to the car thinking of the times she'd admonished Mimi to charge the damn phone and to buy a new car; remembering how Baby Doll, a young prostitute whom Mimi had befriended, had, when she discovered the worth of the classic VW, advised Mimi to sell it and buy herself a real car. Gianna looked at the wreck— weak and tiny and helpless— and her brain shut down. She could not put Mimi in a picture that included this awful mess of a car. She looked at her watch again and hoped that Tim was moving fast because she was about to cheat him out of five minutes of his time. Mimi, who could be injured, could need those five minutes.

Mimi was not injured but she was tired, cold, hungry, and angrier than she'd ever been in her life. She'd spent the night in the top of a barn, in frigid darkness, tied to a chair, while stupid, drunk Trudi's stupid, drunk brother, Jodi, was riding around in, and ultimately destroying, her classic VW. They'd laughed about it, the stupid, drunk siblings, and then had discussed how much they could sell the car's parts and components for. What parts there were remaining.

Mimi had studied them, brother and sister— twins— and had been first amazed by their similarities, and then frightened by them. Certainly they were similar physically: tall, lean, blonde and blue-eyed, with thick, abundant curly hair. Trudi's face, however, was more angular than Jodi's, her mouth a thin line, while her brother's lips were full and beautifully shaped. They'd definitely shared the same egg. And they shared another trait: they were cruel. They enjoyed causing misery to others and they enjoyed watching others in misery. Mimi pitied any pets they might have had as children; pitied any friends they might have had.

They had argued among themselves whether Mimi would be more miserable left alone with bright light shining in her face— the barn was equipped with a generator— or whether the darkness would be more frightening. Mimi refused to give them a hint, so they'd decided on darkness, after agreeing not to let her use the bathroom and taking bets on whether she'd have wet herself by morning. She hadn't, but only by sheer force of will and her own mean streak. She was damned if she'd show weakness to Trudi and Jodi Thompson.

Her resolve wavered when, shortly after sunrise, they returned, dragging Peggy Carter up the wooden ladder to the barn loft, and accompanied by a woman who resembled them enough to be another sibling. Triplets, for crying out loud! The new woman carried a chair and a length of rope and she tied Peggy to it while Peggy begged her to be careful of her hands. Mimi pretended not to know who she was and waited until their captors left to speak to the older woman, who was frightened out of her wits.

Mimi identified herself and, hoping to relax Peggy, explained how she came to be tied up in a barn. Instead, Peggy Carter began to cry and it was some minutes before she could explain herself. And the more Peggy talked— about herself and Sandra Phillips and Trudi— the more despairing Mimi grew.

Until Peggy said through her tears, "I guess I'm really here because that police lieutenant changed her mind."

"What police lieutenant?"

"Maglione is her name and she told me not to tell anybody about my relationship with Sandy but Trudi knew. She hit me just like she hit Sandy and she said she's going to kill me, just like she killed Sandy." Peggy's tears began again, and, for the first time, tears formed in Mimi's eyes. But they were a different kind of tears.

"She didn't change her mind, Peggy."

"How do you know that? You said you've been here since yesterday and I talked to her on Saturday morning. Unless...did you talk to her before you got here?"

"We had an appointment on Saturday afternoon and she cancelled it, and she didn't come home Saturday night and she was still at work Sunday morning. That means she's probably looking for Trudi right now. Probably looking for us." *There has been a development.* Anyway, Mimi though, she doesn't change her mind too often.

Peggy's tears stopped as suddenly as if someone turned off the faucet and she turned as far toward Mimi as her bound hands and feet would allow. "I guess that means is you're on better than mere speaking terms with our pretty lieutenant. And if I were a bit younger, I'd give you a run, Miss Patterson."

Mimi gave Peggy a sideways look. "Given the way you play the piano and sing, you don't need to be a day younger, Miss Carter. Gianna's a sucker for an acoustic piano and a sexy love song."

Peggy sniffed and said archly, "So I've noticed."

It was snowing when Gianna emerged from the copse of trees, flurries, really, so fine and sporadic they hadn't penetrated the tree tops. She stuffed her hands down into her pockets and, keeping her eyes on the barn, walked toward it. Not slowly, not rapidly. She just walked, one foot in front of the other. And when

169

she got to the door it opened and she looked into the same face three times. Stared, really, at the three of them. Tall, lean, beautiful, thick, curly blonde hair, mean blue eyes. Two girls, one boy, the boy a bit thinner and not as attractive but more effeminate than the girls. But those distinctions required close scrutiny, and the time to scrutinize. A quick glance, in the dark, and either of them could be mistaken for the other. She looked at the girls more closely. One of them had longer hair, almost shoulder length, the roots light, the ends much darker. The arm of a pair of tortoise shell glasses stuck out of the pocket of her plaid flannel shirt. This is who Millie was kissing.

Gianna looked into the eyes of the other woman. "You stood me up the other day, Trudi, which really pissed me off. They don't teach good manners where you're from, I guess."

Trudi's eyes widened, then narrowed as recognition took hold. "Who the fuck are you?"

"Don't matter who she is," the boy said, and grabbed Gianna by the arm and yanked her inside. She stumbled and went down to her knees and took a hard kick to the ribs, which flattened her. She lay there for several seconds, letting her eyes adjust to the semi-darkness of the barn, looking for Mimi, for a place where she could be hidden. Then she rolled over to a sitting position and faced her attackers.

"Erin said I'd find you here," she said to Trudi, still ignoring the other two. "And I'd guess that Jackie Marshall, now that she knows about what's happening in her barn, will send you packing again. Might even have you arrested this time, Trudi."

Trudi's foot shot out but Gianna saw it coming and rolled over and quickly up, and began to backpedal. The boy was too good for that. In two strides he was upon her. He snatched her by the arm, whipped it around behind her, grabbed her other arm, and pinned them together in one hand, as if he were handcuffing her. With his other hand he patted her down. He was a cop! It was he who knew that killing their victims in so many different jurisdictions would confuse the police; he was who knew that it

170

would take forever to connect the killings, if ever they were connected. It was this man who had orchestrated a near successful string of serial killings. And now he knew who she was.

"Trudi, you idiot, she's a cop," he said, brandishing her gun and badge. "Now we're fucked."

"I told you we couldn't trust Erin," the other girl said. "She doesn't give a shit about you anymore, Trudi, why can't you get that through your think skull?"

"Fuck the both of you," Trudi said, walking up close to Gianna, so close that Gianna had to tilt her head back and look up to meet her eyes because Trudi was several inches taller. "What did you want with me?"

"To tell you that we found Sandy's correspondence with you, the emails you told her to destroy. She didn't, just like she didn't do most of what you told her to do. She'd hidden all your little love notes in a folder behind some books. You searched her place, or maybe the officer back here searched, but you missed it." Gianna winced as the boy behind her tightened his grip on her arms and pulled up.

"Damn it, Trudi!" the other girl whispered, "I told you she was wrong from the beginning. I *knew* she was wrong, I just knew it. She wasn't like the others. I told you that, but you wouldn't listen, and now look at the mess we're in."

A nauseous rage welled up within Gianna. Not only did these people target and victimize women, they traded them back and forth like game pieces. This is the girl who was kissing Millie and wooing Sandy, not Trudi. Or maybe they took turns.

Trudi whirled around to face her. "Shut up, Ursula!" She turned back to Gianna and Gianna was ready for her.

"And that wasn't your only mistake, Trudi. You all are pretty good, but Mr. Macho back here isn't as good a cop as he thinks he is or he wouldn't have washed out. And you did wash out, didn't you? Not smart enough? Not able to follow orders? Don't play well with others?"

The snatch up on her arms this time made her cry out and

171

she dropped to her knees, bringing him down with her. She tried to twist out of his grip but this was no drunken Irishman, slipping and sliding on the ice. He gut-punched her and she went limp, which earned her another kick in the ribs. She didn't know how much more time she could buy Tim and unless he could get into the barn without being seen, he wouldn't be much help alone anyway. And at this rate, she wouldn't be much help to him.

"We gotta get outta here," Ursula said. "Trudi, you hear? I've had enough of your little game. You paid 'em back, you got even, now let's go! I'm not going to jail because you think you got a golden pussy."

Behind Gianna, the boy snickered. "She's right, Trud, enough's enough. And I ain't gonna kill no cop, golden pussy or not."

"What difference does it make? It's just one more."

"It's a *cop*, you stupid cunt! Let's tie her up and leave her here with the other two, and let's get outta here. We got more than enough money and stuff now."

Gianna's breath caught in her chest. She was inhaling when he jerked her up and the surprise of hearing that there were two hostages almost choked her— Mimi and who else?

"I'm not leaving that old bitch alive, you hear me, Jodi? We can't leave her alive. I can't let two women dump me for old bitches, you know I can't do that! Don't make me do that, Jodi!"

Trudi was sobbing hysterically. She'd transformed from a snarling menace to a slobbering mess in an instant, her speech virtually unintelligible as she moaned about two old bitches taking her women from her, one of them Black.

Peggy Carter? Had to be. Gianna inhaled deeply and then exhaled deeply. Slowly and rhythmically, she inhaled and exhaled several times more, clearing her mind, easing the pain of the new punches and kicks as they increased the pain of those from the day before, compliments of an Irish gunrunner.

Peggy was being held hostage with Mimi, somewhere in the darkness of the barn, waiting for Gianna to devise some kind

172

of plan to free them. But there was no possibility of that; she was as trapped as they were. Jodi had her weapon and most likely one of his own. She didn't think Trudi or Ursula had weapons but she couldn't be certain. She couldn't be certain of anything except that Mimi possibly was injured and that Peggy Carter was sixty years old and possibly injured as well.

"Fuck a duck," she muttered.

"What did she say?"

Jodi giggled behind her. "She said, 'fuck a duck.' I haven't heard anybody say that in years. Knew a dude from Australia used to say that. You from Australia?" Jodi pulled up on her arms to indicate that he expected an answer and Gianna shook her head. "Where, then?"

"Philadelphia," she said, and all hell broke loose.

Gunfire, an explosion, blaring horns, shouts, and screams, all at once. Gianna twisted free of Jodi, dropped to the ground, and scurried off on all fours, though she wasn't certain that she was evading danger since the noise that filled the barn seemed to come from everywhere all at once.

"Police! Everybody freeze!"

"Police officer! Nobody move!"

Tim and Linda. Gianna obeyed the order and didn't move, wouldn't move until she knew what was happening, but she did open her eyes. Daylight was pouring into the barn, compliments of the big Chevy Suburban that had created a new door at the rear. Tim McCreedy was standing on top of it firing his Glock into the air.

Gianna looked toward the front of the barn just as the door opened a crack, letting one of the tall, lean bodies slip out. She struggled to her feet and sprinted to the front door and out. Already the runner was thirty yards away, high stepping through the stalks. Gianna guessed it was Jodi and she knew she'd never catch him so she turned back to the barn and, utilizing the sliver of space in the open door, she slithered back in. Tim no longer was on top of the truck, she didn't know where Linda was, and it was deadly silent inside. Gianna merged into a shadow on the wall and stood there, regulating her breath.

Suddenly the Suburban's lights went on, illuminating everything in front of the truck. Gianna scanned the area. Linda had one of the women pinned to the floor, handcuffing her. She crawled over to them and looked at the woman. It was Ursula. Nobody else on the floor and no place for anyone to hide. She looked up. Nothing on three walls. A second floor running the length of the barn on the far side, a wooden ladder leading upward mid-way the wall. The lights went out and Gianna remained where she was, waiting for Tim to come to her.

"Are you all right?" he whispered, and when she nodded, he asked if she still had her weapon. Then he asked if she knew where it was, and the three of them shared a moment of regret at her negative response. It never went down well when a cop lost a weapon to a perp.

"Mimi and Peggy Carter are upstairs in that loft and Mimi may be hurt and I think Trudi Thompson is up there with them."

Linda asked, "How in hell are we going to get up there without getting nailed? Does she have your weapon?"

Gianna shook her head and Tim shook his, though for a different reason. "That business with the truck was my last, best trick, Boss."

Gianna looked up at the loft. Trudi and maybe a length of piano wire and a few minutes to herself. She sprinted for the wooden ladder. Tim and Linda followed. She stopped at the bottom, turned and whispered, "When I'm halfway up, start shooting, and then follow." Her last best trick was to hope that Trudi was still unraveled and that the wild firing of guns so near would bring her the rest of the way unglued.

The screaming began almost immediately. Gianna scrambled up the ladder as fast as she could, oblivious to the splinters she was gathering along the way. Trudi was at the top of the stairs, hands over her ears, screeching and mumbling. Gianna knocked her down and pinned her to the floor until Eric and

174

Linda could subdue her. She was still screaming and sobbing when the ambulance arrived.

So was Peggy Carter. She said she'd rather not have learned that Sandy was leaving Trudi to be with her. Knowing that she'd lost her last chance at love was worse than not having had it, she said. There was no song that gave words to her feelings and Peggy Carter said she knew all the lost love songs.

Mimi was so angry she was rigid. Gianna had untied her and, after making certain she was uninjured, helped her down the ladder. She refused, as did Peggy, to play it safe and accept ambulance transport to the hospital. Peggy stretched out in the back seat of the Chevy Suburban that still was parked in the middle of the garage. Gianna walked Mimi outside to get some air, and to get her calm and rational enough to talk. She said she wasn't hurt or scared. She was mad.

"That little bastard destroyed my car and he and his sorry-ass sister laughed about it! I'd like to get my hands around their sick, disgusting necks and squeeze until I can't hold on any longer."

"Did he say anything, Mimi--"

"He said he was going to sell the parts off my car!"

Gianna grabbed her by both arms and gently shook her until her eyes focused. "Jodi got away and I need you to tell me if he said anything that could help us find him."

Mimi rubbed her wrists where they had been bound and tied to the chair. She touched Gianna's face. "I think they were going to kill me."

Gianna held her and she shivered. "Let's go back in."

Mimi shook her head. "They talked about going to Texas. They did it for the money, Gianna. They killed those women so they could steal their assets. That's why they got them to move here and to buy new furniture and cars and clothes. They've got all that stuff and they're going to move to Texas." Mimi shivered again and Gianna thought she could be going into shock.

"You need to be checked by a doctor, Mimi," she said.

"I'm all right, Gianna. I haven't been dropped or hit on the head and I'm not in shock. I'm just mad. And...and sad.'

"Hey Boss!" Tim came galloping around the corner of the barn. "They've got him! The stupid fuck went home. Shit for brains, huh?"

"Glad he's not one of ours," Gianna said.

"He's on the job?" Tim was incredulous.

Gianna shook her head. "Not any more." To Mimi she said, "I've got to get you home. Tim, would you--"

"Got it covered, Boss," he said, offering Mimi his arm. "My pleasure, Miss Patterson."

"It won't be if I don't get to a bathroom," she snapped, crossing her legs.

CHAPTER TWELVE

Mimi's exclusive front page story on the arrest of the three Thompsons for the murders of six women over the last two years restored her to favor with the higher-ups at the paper. Even the Weasel expressed his admiration. So pleased was he, in fact, that he didn't flinch when she asked to do follow-up stories that would focus on menopause and society's treatment of women "of a certain age" and how that treatment may have led to the Thompson's almost getting away with murder.

DOES MENOPAUSE KILL? was the headline of the first story. The first paragraphs read:

> *It is ancient, older than civilization itself, the time when women cease experiencing their monthly menstrual cycles. It is called menopause and it is not a single event but a process, a series of events and changes that can take longer than a decade to complete. The majority of women don't know this, though every one of them will experience this process if they live long enough. What women seem to know is that menopause is something to be hated, feared, resented, resisted, reviled. And why not, asks 53-three year old Phyllis, who also asks that her last name not be used. "It's an ugly word. My mother and grandmother and aunts called everything to do with female bodily functions 'the curse.' And now I'm supposed to embrace something*

that sounds so ugly and does such
ugly things to my body?"
The word, menopause, is Greek
in origin, and means "to bring an
end to the moon," or monthly
cycle. Some of the effects on the
female body include weight gain,
loss of libido, night sweats, brittle
nails, thinning head hair, growth
of facial hair. Some of the effects
on the female psyche are much
more subtle and perhaps even
dangerous.

The public response to Mimi's story was immediate and overwhelming. The phone lines were jammed. Email to the paper and to Mimi caused the system to shut down for over an hour. Every television news channel in town rushed to do similar stories. Clinics and hospitals were overrun with requests for information on menopause, and therapists were bombarded with requests for appointments from previously silent women wanting to talk about what was happening to them, many of them under the mistaken impression that they'd either imagined what they were feeling, that it was unique or unusual, or that there was nothing anybody could do about it. And that was the positive response. The negative response was as vociferous if not plentiful. The detractors found the stories lurid, unchristian, even Satanic.

"Looks like you touched an exposed nerve," Tyler said, stopping at her desk the morning after the second menopause story ran. "Way to go, Patterson," he said, actually shaking her hand as if she'd won some kind of prize. "You may be free at last of government graft and corruption for a while. The bosses are happy."

Which didn't mean very much to Mimi at the moment. She was happier about the phone call she'd just received from Sue.

178

She'd emailed Sue and Kate all the articles and Kate finally had opened up and expressed her feelings: she saw herself as fat and balding and not at all sexually attractive. "She's got an appointment with a therapist and a doctor," Sue said. "I think we're going to be all right, Mimi."

But not everybody was pleased with her. Alice Long was not. Mimi had kept their Wednesday evening appointment at *The Bayou*, intending to tell Alice who she really was and why she'd been at *Happy Landings*, and to tell her that friendship would be the extent of any relationship that might develop between them. Alice already knew.

"I'd figured you were more than a day tripper," was her opening greeting. "But a *reporter*! Damn!"

"Ouch, Alice, lighten up," Mimi said. "Everybody's got to earn a living. And there are lots of people who don't think much of cops, so be careful about disparaging other people's professions. Besides, it could always be worse. We could be lawyers."

The levity was lost on Alice. "But you're not one of those people who thinks badly of cops, are you Miss Patterson? Especially if the cop is a lieutenant."

Mimi hadn't asked how Alice knew about Gianna; it didn't matter how she knew. What mattered was that Gianna didn't know that Alice knew and Mimi needed to tell her. She kept waiting for the right moment. That hadn't happened yet. Gianna's post-Thompson experience had been a bit rockier than Mimi's.

Gianna looked at the chief and realized that she didn't know when she'd stopped listening to him, when she'd stopped caring what he had to say. Despite Mimi's half dozen articles, despite Peggy Carter's appearance on four national television news and entertainment programs, despite the very public gratitude of three different law enforcement agencies, politicians in D.C. still managed to blame Lieutenant Maglione and the Hate Crimes Unit— and, by extension, the chief of police— for violating all kinds of jurisdictional and procedural rules and regulations in the apprehension and arrest of Trudi and Jodi Thompson and their cousin, Ursula. No points for the painstaking piecing together of evidence that linked the three Thompsons to six murders. No pats on the back for finally identifying two Jane Does, the first two victims, and returning them to their families. And no credit given to Gianna and Hate Crimes for preventing a cache of automatic weapons from making its way across the Atlantic to Ireland; the SWAT people got the credit for that one.

Three weeks after the fact and the anti-Hate Crimes faction on the City Council was out for Gianna's blood. What upset the politicians was their inability to force her to acknowledge that she'd made the procedural errors, and to apologize in public. So, in the middle of the budget meeting, with the Hate Crimes Unit appropriation on the line, the most hostile city council member repeated what he'd heard on a TV news program: that Gianna first learned about the missing lesbians while at a lesbian bar, and he asked if that were true. Gianna asked him what difference it made who told her about the missing women or where. The councilman then asked Gianna if she frequented lesbian bars. She told him it was none of his business what kind of bars, if any, she frequented. Sensing immediately where things were headed and determined to steer a different path, a friendly council member asked Gianna what church she attended. She refused to answer that question, as well as others inquiring about the make and model of her personal car and whether she owned or rented her living space and whether she kept pets. Not only was it none of their business, Gianna told them, but it had no bearing on the quality or effectiveness of her service to the District of Columbia Police Department.

The chief of police was livid and had been expressing his feelings for the last eternity, it seemed. Gianna didn't care. She stood up so abruptly that he stopped talking in the middle of a word. "You going somewhere?"

"Yes sir. I'm going to the gym and I'm going to be late

for my massage if I don't leave now."

"Maglione..." The warning in his voice was ominous.

"I've done my best for you, sir, and I'm sorry if it hasn't been sufficient. I'm sorry the city council is so...so...whatever it is they are. And I'm truly sorry that you have to dance when they pull the strings, but I don't have to."

"Yes, dammit, you do, Maglione, and that's what I've been trying to get you to understand since I gave you Hate Crimes!" He got up and walked around his desk to stand close to her. "Running a unit is a political assignment and you're judged by how well you play the game, not by how many perps you lock up. That's all I've been trying to get you to understand."

She heard the pleading in his voice, saw in his eyes how much he wanted her acquiescence. And somewhere deep within, she wanted to give in, to accept, to capitulate. She could not. Her father, the Philadelphia street cop shot down because it was assumed that with an Italian surname he was Mafia, would not have understood and she'd have no words to explain. "I appreciate your trust and confidence. If I'm a good cop, it's because you taught me well. And if I'm a bad politician, it's because my father taught me well. He was the first good cop I knew and if I have to choose which one of you to follow, then I choose him." She walked across his office to the door, her feet making no sound and dragging slightly in the plush carpet.

"Maglione." He hit the "g" harder than usual, it seemed, and she turned around to face him, one hand on the door knob. He held her gaze for a long few seconds. "A massage. That sounds like a good idea."

****

"Tyler's attack dog isn't finished with the City Council yet," Mimi said through a yawn she didn't try to stifle, "so don't worry too much about what those clowns are doing. Most of 'em can't find their butts with their own two hands anyway. And the chief'll settle down soon, too, don't you think?"

Gianna opened one eye and peered at Mimi through the

steam. There already had been two stories in the paper detailing the overwhelmingly negative public response to the city council's treatment of Gianna, and Gianna's steadfast refusal to add any comment of her own had done nothing to reduce the apparent public and community support she enjoyed. "What does that mean, exactly?" she asked, unable to conceal the trepidation in her voice, "that Tyler's 'attack dog' isn't finished? Or is that something I probably don't want to know?"

"Well," Mimi drawled, "it seems that Councilman I-Hate-Dykes was stupid enough to have an unregistered lobbyist on his staff and on his payroll. That's a few kinds of illegal. You can read all about that in tomorrow's paper, along with a story about some unusual deposits to his bank account." Mimi yawned again and stretched full out on the bench. "God will bless whoever invented massages and steam chambers."

"Did you tell Tyler that stuff about the councilman?"

Instead of answering the question, Mimi said, "By the way, Trimble's wife dropped her lawsuit when her lawyer got a look at the countersuit the paper was considering, so that's a worry I don't have to sweat. I can just lie here in the steam and sweat naturally and normally instead of emotionally."

"You didn't answer my question," Gianna said.

"And you can't really think the chief is going to fire you," Mimi said through a yawn. "And yeah, I gave Tyler that stuff about the councilman, though he could have found out on his own. It's been City Hall gossip for a couple of weeks."

"How do you know? You haven't been near City Hall for months."

"Sources," Mimi said. "How many times do I have to tell you that we reporters have sources just like cops; probably even better ones."

Gianna shrugged and stretched out on the other bench and hoped nobody else came in so they wouldn't have to sit up and make room, happy to let that subject drop and switch to another one. "You earn enough money to keep us both, don't you? Just in case I do get fired."

"Not any more. I had to buy a new car, remember?"

"But you didn't have to buy such an expensive one!"

Mimi snorted. "You're the one who was just dying for a convertible with power everything and that off-the-wall color that there isn't even a name for that had to be specially ordered from the factory. Not to mention the built-in car phone. And if the damn thing doesn't come soon, I'm getting my deposit back."

"No, you're not and don't change the subject. Suppose I am fired...."

"Will I keep you in the style to which you've grown accustomed? Sure," Mimi said. "You don't really eat that much and you're a great cook and you're really good about picking up after yourself, although your taste in movies sucks."

"But if there's only one mortgage to pay," Gianna said sleepily, "two can probably live as cheaply as one, and we can take turns with movies."

Mimi sat up and looked down at Gianna, who appeared to be asleep. She had positively refused to entertain the notion of their living together. Mimi had her house in D.C. and Gianna had her condo in Silver Spring and that was that. Was she proposing that they live together? Was that contingent on her being fired from her job? Where would they live? Would Mimi have to sell her house? She was trying to decide which question to ask first when the door swung open and Phyllis, Dot, Evie and June sailed in on a wave of commentary. Gianna, eyes still closed, grinned. She'd gotten to know and like them.

"Wake up, Lieutenant, no rest for the weary," Phyllis trilled, and leered as Gianna sat up. "How long do I have to spend on that chest press machine to get my boobs to do that?"

"You could take up residence on the chest press machine and your boobs wouldn't do that," Evie said with an admiring glance at Gianna's breasts.

"Behave yourselves," Mimi admonished, trying to stifle a giggle and sound stern as she moved over and made room for

183

them to sit.

"We've started a recall campaign against that homophobe on the City Council," Dot said. "We've already got five hundred signatures. He's at-large so you can sign, Mimi. Too bad you can't, Gianna."

"She wouldn't if she could, would you?" June asked.

Gianna smiled noncommittally but made no comment.

"And as for you," Phyllis said with a menacing look at Mimi and attaching hands to hips.

"As for me what? What did I do now?" Mimi winced as if expecting a blow.

"You opened that Pandora's Box of questions and issues and then didn't give us all the answers, that's what you did. I still don't know if menopause is what killed those women, and I still don't know whether I should just accept these extra ten or twenty pounds or if I should keep going to the gym, trying to get rid of them."

Mimi sighed. "In the first place, it's not my job to give you all the answers. If you're smart enough and interested enough to read a daily newspaper, you're smart enough to find your own answers and reach your own conclusions."

"That's a cop-out," Dot said.

"No it's not," Mimi countered. "If I tell you what to think then it's *my* belief, *my* value system you're following and not your own, and that's both wrong and stupid."

"Humph," Phyllis said.

"And come on, Phyllis, be real. Of course menopause didn't kill those women, Trudi and Jodi and Ursula Thompson killed them—"

"That's another cop-out," Dot said.

"No it's not," Mimi and Gianna said in unison.

"But they wouldn't have been killed if they hadn't been going through the change, isn't that right?" Dot asked.

"There's sufficient physical and forensic evidence to tie the Thompsons to six murders and no, I won't tell you what that evidence is," Gianna said, wishing she could tell them, especially about the piece of jewelry belonging to each murdered woman that investigators found in Trudi's luggage. "So it doesn't matter whether they were experiencing menopause."

"But Mimi said it did!"

"No I didn't," Mimi said. "I asked whether it was possible that the view we have of menopause, and therefore of ourselves, is so overwhelmingly negative that an otherwise sane and rational woman would accept a sight-unseen declaration of love because she believed that would be her last chance at love. I asked the question. I did not supply an answer because *my* answer would be *my* answer. It's every woman for herself, and I'm certain that somewhere today a woman is falling in love over the internet, in a chat room, because the truth is, you never know where or when you'll find love."

And both Mimi and Gianna recalled that they'd found it in this very steam room less than two years ago.

"So true," Evie said, "so, so, true," ending the reflective moment. "Do you know how true, Mimi?"

"I'll bet you're going to tell me."

"Oh, don't be coy, Evie," June said. "Tell her."

"We-ll-l," Evie said, drawing out the word, "that Alice you introduced me to--"

"What Alice?" Gianna said, now fully alert.

"Her name's Alice Long," Phyllis said, "and you should see her! That girl is so fine she hurts your eyes! And next time you have somebody to introduce, Mimi, make it to me."

"I didn't know you knew Alice," Gianna said to Mimi.

"We've met," Mimi said, eliciting guffaws from the other four women.

"Don't worry, Gianna, honey," Evie said in that same slow drawl and sounding a lot like Alice. "I promise you that I'm the only one Officer Long has eyes for these days, and from what I can see Miss Patterson has eyes only for you. So relax, Girl."

Gianna stood up and extended a hand to Mimi. "Come

on," she said.

Mimi took Gianna's hand and stood up. "Where are we going?"

"To get the real estate section from the paper. You've got to find us a place to live and it's got to have an attached garage and a hot tub. And how is it you know Alice Long well enough to introduce her to somebody?"

An excerpt from *KEEPING SECRETS*
the first Mimi Patterson/Gianna Maglione Mystery
To be reissued by **migibooks** February, 2002.

Mimi thumbed through the stacks of files about outing piled on top of her desk, alternating between anger and dismay. How could one gay person not understand, not respect, the unwillingness or the inability of another to come out? Being queer in America, she thought wryly, was one of the few things worse than being Black. It was possible to be forgiven the color of one's skin, the assumption being that one had no choice in the matter. But to love one's same sex—that was something else. No matter how hotly the debate raged in medical and scientific circles, a significant portion of the population seemed to think that gay people needed only to decide to stop being gay and that was that. Mimi didn't know of a single person who had delighted in informing his or her family/friends/colleagues/ clients/ patients/ landlord/employer of the fact of his or her gayness. She sighed and tossed the files aside. In terms of the investigation she'd been assigned, outers outraged people but they didn't kill them.

She paged through the file she'd compiled on the four murder victims. The twenty-first day of July, August, September and October—Murray, delValle, Grayson and Tancil, killed in that order. They'd all married in their twenties, either before understanding the truth of their sexuality or believing that a conventional marriage was the only option. They had all lived in the wealthiest sections of the Maryland and Virginia suburbs that surrounded Washington, but each was murdered far from home, in a darkened parking lot or garage inside the city.

She tossed the files aside in irritation. What she had was virtually nothing and what she needed was hard information. She reached for the phone, hesitated, then resolutely dialed.

"Lieutenant Maglione, please. This is Montgomery Patterson." Her heart rate increased when the composed voice answered.

"Miss Patterson. How can I help?"

She's so remote, Mimi thought. Maybe somebody's with her. "Can you tell me, please, Lieutenant, how Mrs. Grayson, Mr. Tancil, Mr. Murray and Mr. delValle, all happened to be in those parking lots so late at night?"

There was the slightest pause before Gianna responded. "I'm afraid you have me at a disadvantage, Miss Patterson, since only you know what you're talking about."

Mimi smiled in spite of herself. You're good, Lieutenant. Very good. "Will you at least tell me how much longer you think we'll have to play games with each other about this case?"

"I take it you mean the case I haven't acknowledged exists?"

"You can acknowledge its existence or I can file an FOI for access to the case information," Mimi snapped. "Tell me what you'd like me to do, Lieutenant."

"I'd like for you to have a very pleasant day, Miss Patterson."

Gianna winced and jerked the phone away from her ear as Mimi slammed it down on the other end. She smile wanly at Eric who was seated across the desk, feet up, eating a turkey sandwich and reading the lab report on the Tancil car. Gianna rotated her neck, hoping to release the knot of tension that seemed to have taken up permanent residence.

"A reporter somehow knows about Grayson, Tancil, et al."

Eric got sandwich caught in his throat and coughed before he could speak. "Knows? Knows what? Knows they were all gay? How is that possible?"

"I don't know how she knows, but Montgomery Patterson is privy to that information. I can only be thankful that if a reporter must know, it's her. At least she won't rush to print without all the facts. Have a set of purged files delivered to her."

"You really want to give her the files?" he asked incredulously.

188

"I'm just giving her what she already knows and I'd rather do that than have her arousing interest by filing a Freedom of Information Act request. Every reporter in town would jump on that bandwagon."

Eric tossed her a half salute and ambled out. She sat quietly, thinking about Mimi Patterson. Sooner or later they'd have to talk about the case. More precisely, Gianna would have to divulge facts in order to find out what the reporter knew and from what source. She'd never had much dealing with the press and she had been warned that her promotion would change all that. At least half the job of heading up a major crimes unit, the chief had told her, was public relations.

But she hadn't figured on M. Montgomery Patterson. She pushed the image of Mimi out of her mind, Mimi naked, her smooth, burnished umber skin so close to her, the heat between them not all from the steam room. She closed her eyes to Mimi and opened them to the files before her, to the horrible, depraved, ugliness that would consume her until she found and stopped him-her-those responsible.

What in these files would lead her to the killer? What, if anything, did she—the officer in charge of the investigation— know that Mimi Patterson, the reporter, did not know? Not a hell of a lot. That Phil Tancil's wife had become hysterical when confronted with her husband's homosexuality, and so angry that Gianna had feared being assaulted by her. She'd refused to discuss it, refused to permit a search of his personal belongings, accused the police of tarnishing the image of a good family man, and called her lawyer when Gianna obtained a search warrant. She could not and would not understand why the police needed to know the tiniest details of a victim's background in order to find his killer, and she refused to join any speculation about the reason for his presence in the Washington High School parking lot well after midnight on a Monday night.

Joe Murray's wife had responded in exactly the opposite manner. Eerily calm, she told Gianna she'd known Joe was hiding

189

something, and that he was carrying some weight that often made him aloof and distant for long periods of time. Her worst fear, she told Gianna, was that Joe was engaged in some illegal activity, because she hadn't fully understood that her husband's consulting firm was as successful as he claimed it was, and she'd wondered where all the money came from. She allowed Gianna and her team full access to Joe's home and office safes where he kept his private papers, but insisted that the Murray children know nothing of their father's homosexuality. Why would Joe Murray be in the deserted, cavernous parking lot of RFK Stadium at midnight? "He loved the Redskins," she said with a resigned shrug. And did she believe, Gianna had asked gently, that Joe's murder could be sexually oriented? "It would appear so," she'd answered with painful honesty.

Tony delValle's wife was angry. She'd know of her husband's homosexuality for years. They'd seen therapists together and separately and Tony would give up men for a while, but only for a while, until the AIDS scare, and she had believed Tony's promise that he was "out of the life for good." He'd said he was afraid of AIDS, and he knew that his habit of meeting men in bars and movie houses endangered himself and his family. "And now I find out in the worse way that he lied to me." She spat out the words.

Gianna probed, "So, you think your husband's murder was tied to his sexual activities?"

The woman's pain and anger boiled over. "He was driving a forty thousand dollar car. He was wearing five thousand dollars worth of jewelry. He had almost five hundred dollars in his pocket. Do you think I'm stupid, Lady? Whoever killed him didn't do it for money!" Gianna accepted the full force of the woman's fury because she could do no less.

It was Liz Grayson's husband who gave Gianna the first bit of information that resembled a lead. Harry Grayson, a tall, thin, handsome man in his late forties, longish hair almost totally silver, had known for years of his wife's attraction to and involvement with women, but he also knew that she was much to conventional to try and face the world without her husband and children. They were her protection, her insulation, and she would do nothing to jeopardize that. She was not promiscuous, he insisted, but rather engaged in long-term affairs, most recently with Susan Jolley, a computer analyst for the Army. They'd stopped seeing each other about a month before Liz was killed, he said, because of threats made by Susan's ex-lover, a woman named Karen.

"What kind of threats, Mr. Grayson?"
She touched his arm as tears filled his eyes, spilled down his cheeks.

He removed the silver-edged half glasses and allowed the tears to   flow unchecked. The navy   corduroy slacks and turtleneck sweater he wore perfectly complimented the image of the research scientist that he was. "The kind I now know to take seriously. This Karen threatened to kill Liz because she thought Liz took Susan away from her."

Harry Grayson looked helplessly around the homey den filled with soft, rich furniture and photographs of himself and his wife and their children and other family members. "I can't believe she's gone, Lieutenant." And he wiped tears with the back of his hand.

Susan Jolley was also gone, had disappeared. Quit her job, sold her car, emptied her bank account, and vanished. These little bit of information the police investigator did not share with the investigative reporter; instead she stingily kept them close, guarding them, in case one of the bits ripened and bore fruit--the hard, bitter fruit that leads, eventually and ultimately, to a murderer.

"You've only been on the story a week and a half, Patterson. What makes you think you should have all the answers already? Starting to believe your own press?"

"Tyler, I can't even get the Hate Crimes Unit to admit

they're working the case."

"There's your proof."

"Proof of what!" Mimi snapped. "I don't even know what I'm looking for."

"You're looking for who's killing gay people."

"That's not my job! There's an extremely competent, not to mention extremely gorgeous, police lieutenant whose job it is to find murderers."

Tyler said very quietly, "Don't you care?"

"Of course I care," she said wearily, "but the more I dig into this case, the more I find that what I want to know is why. I want to know how it happens that a person hates enough to kill."

Thank you for choosing a Mimi Patterson/
Gianna Maglione Mystery from **migibooks**.
We hope you enjoyed it and that you will
want to have all the Mimi/Gianna books in
your library. Visit our website to find the
bookstore nearest you that stocks the Mimi/
Gianna books, or buy them directly from us.

LOVE NOTES   *$12.95*
KEEPING SECRETS   *$12.95*
NIGHT SONGS   *$ 12.95*
Plus applicable tax, shipping and handling.

Order by mail: *migibooks*
                 PO Box 20365
                 Los Angeles, CA 90006

Order by phone: *1.866.GET-MIGI (438-6444)*

Visit our website and
Order online: **www.migibooks.com**

193